Mystery and Fantasy in Christchurch, Dorset.

CW01024338

Jemima's Circus

Adventures in Dorset.

Glenn Edgeley-Long

Mystery and Fantasy in Christchurch, Dorset.

DEDICATION

To the younger members of my family – Rosie; Colby; Rupert; Jack; Jemima; Alex; Ananda; Elias; Avery and Elowen, also Mix and Mint.

And all those who consider themselves to be - **'young at heart'.**

Mystery and Fantasy in Christchurch, Dorset.

Contents

Jemima's Circus Adventures

In Dorset

Jemima Jones carrying cousin Elowen

Mystery and Fantasy in Christchurch, Dorset.

ACKNOWLEDGMENTS

To Master Ananda Edgeley-Long
who helped me check the contents of this book.

Mystery and Fantasy in Christchurch, Dorset.

Chapter One

A stormy night and a strange man.

Across the darkened marshes close to the entrance of Christchurch harbour on the Dorset coast, an old man is desperately trying to see his way ahead. Standing up in the front of a small sailing boat and holding onto the slender mast to steady himself against the cold wind, he places his hands over his eyes to protect them from the fierce gale blowing across the hostile nearby marshes. With no moon to light his way and only the nighttime stars to guide him, he shudders as all he sees is the flat marshy ground of the unforgiving marshes to his right. To his left, as he tries to see something he might recognise, the wind blows into his face causing him to further cover his eyes. Managing to make out trees against a hill, he thinks he might be close to Hengistbury Head. Calling out to the small figure huddled in the rear of the small craft, he shouts, "ahead, ahead," as the wind carries his voice across the water.

"Sir," calls out a frightened voice from the rear of the small craft. "I cannot control the rudder with this strong wind and with the water hereabouts being so shallow, we will surely be aground and left for cutthroats that do infest these marshes who will surely end our days, should they find us here."

"We must go on, we are not safe here," called out the old man as he still struggled to see the way ahead in the darkness.

"Smugglers sir, this area is known throughout all of Dorset for the smuggling in this harbour and this night be too foul for customs men to venture thus far. Tis such a night those that run contraband do prefer. If they do see us, they will attack us for sure and then take what little we have."

Looking again to his right to see the lie of the land, the old man again shouted, cupping his hand to his mouth to make himself heard, "to the right then, there be marshland that is risen higher than the rest hereabouts and they that smuggle venture not there. Turn your rudder that I may make for those trees beyond these marshes. There shall I find firm ground and shelter."

"Abbott Joshua, Abbott Joshua," called out a frightened voice, "what sir of the Priory?" the huddled figure strained to make himself heard against the strong wind. "Tis ahead, I can see the tower and the monks do offer you a meal and a bed. Tis not far, but I must take to the middle of the river if we are to avoid these shallow marshes. If smugglers be out this night, that be where they make their way along the river. They are treacherous and we will surely be seen if we continue as close to them as we shall be. Our throats will be cut by those murdering smugglers who do know this harbour and marshes well enough. They know the paths to take and those places to avoid where might a man be swallowed deep into the soft ground below him should he set a foot upon it."

"Tis a danger I wish to avoid," shouted back the reply. "The Priory tower I now also see, but with hidden dangers on such a darkened night, I must seek shelter elsewhere this night and journey by the light of day to the priory on the morrow."

"Carry things of value upon your person, good sir? A stranger who is out on these marshes on such a night will be looking to enrich himself by the end of the night."

"Turn your rudder that I might get through these pools and towards that raised ground I see a short distance yonder. There may I land and must seek shelter through this stormy night."

"No bed for you this night, sir? Tis folly to be in the open on such a night as this. The power of the wind does even now bend those yonder trees."

"Those trees shall shelter me slightly. Better that than being out on a cruel night with the gale blowing across these marshes and cutting down any in it's way."

"Sir, I can only take you a short distance further, less the craft become stuck in this mud and with no help to make it become free."

Slowly the craft flowed into a small pool against which the nearby grassy bank rose slightly higher.

"Tis here Sir, a short leap and on land you will be, but if it be dry or wet, that I cannot tell in this darkness."

"If it be firm, then shall I make my way to where I may shelter til this storm does blow itself out and on the morrow, journey onto the Priory." As the old man carefully stepped over the side of the small craft and onto the slippery land, he called back, "sail you now back with great care towards the harbour mouth and then close to the coast until you do reach our Priory on the river Hamble.

Under the darkened sky with the wind seeming to become faster still, the old man struggled across the marsh carrying just a small bundle wrapped in sacking. Slowly and with difficulty, he made his way across the soggy ground until he reached the mild shelter he hoped the trees might offer. There he settled himself down against the trunk of the widest tree and under a branch he thought might provide him with some shelter. Very close to him a rabbit emerged from a burrow, eyed the stranger with curiosity, then scampered back into the safety of his dry burrow. Thinking he had placed his small bundle beside him, the old man closed his eyes, hoping he would live to see the sun rise the following day. Further across the marshes, a group of smugglers were making their way with their carts of smuggled goods along a higher part of the marshes and towards the George Inn in the small ancient town of Christchurch.

Early the next morning while the old man still slept, the storm had blown itself out and the morning sun shone brightly, rising across the marshes as three strange looking persons, after an early morning trip to Mudeford Quay to fish, wandered past the trees on their way back to join their circus. Seeing a small wrapped parcel on the grass close to the trees and wondering what it might be, one bent down to pick it up. Undoing the sacking surrounding the item and holding it up, he exclaimed, "a strange object, not one I ever have before did see. Wonder how it got here. The strong winds of last night must have carried it from somewhere close by."

"Nor me neither seen anything like it," said another of the group. "Perhaps someone dropped it as they struggled to get home during the storm last night. It has a strange shape and those dial things do baffle me and those strange things flashing as they are. Best leave it where you found it, might be dangerous, might even explode."

"What about Madame Shavtof, the circus clairvoyant," added the third man. "If anyone would know about it, surely it would be Madame Shavtof. She would know if it would explode or not. Not much Madame Shavtof don't not know about."

Looking at it more closely, the first man agreed. "We'll take it to Madame Shavtof and if she don't know, then nobody else do know, so then we dump it."

"What about we sell it?" added the second man, a man who was shorter than the other two.

"Can't sell it, if no-one know what it be," the man holding the object said. "Best we do as Bertrum suggests, Madame Shavtof or the bin."

"Madame Shavtof or the bin," they all agreed.

Satisfied they had agreed the correct thing to do, with the taller of the three holding the item, they strode off along the narrow path towards the large area close to the village of Christchurch, where a circus and a fair would be held during the coming summer season.

"Jemima," the voice called from outside my bedroom door with an accompanying loud knock, waking me. The storm of the last evening had woken me twice during the night and I worried I would oversleep and not be up early enough to catch sight of a rare bird, reported to be visiting the Stanpit marshes. After that, if there was time, I wanted to visit Mudeford Quay to see the new lifeboat, delivered just a few days ago and due in the water at a certain hour. I hoped the launch would not be cancelled due to any damage caused by the strong winds of the night. Having had a rushed breakfast, I left the house and made my way across the area known in the village as Stanpit Rec, earlier than I had ever been previously. Arriving in good time, I was struck by the sight as I walked across the rec of an old man, stooping slightly and seeming to be searching for something. I did wonder if he had lost a dog as this part of the marsh is a favourite with dog walkers.

"Young Missy," he called over to me as the path brought me closer to him.

Not saying anything, I thought best to walk quickly by, but then noticed his clothes. A tall man, but bending over, probably due to old age. He was dressed from head to foot in a long coat, buttoned up at the front, with a pointed hood covering most of his head.

"Missy, Missy," he again called, "I am in a quandary. Your assistance would be appreciated. I am searching and have been searching, but my searches have not found that with which I have been entrusted."

"Sir?" I answered. I could not think of anything else to say.

6

"The storm of the night has caused me to become confused. Trying to find shelter, I thought I had left an item of great value, very close to me. Now it is not where I thought I had left it. I am fearful an animal might have carried it off."

Still wondering what to say, at last I thought to ask, "sir, what is it you have lost?"

"It is not here or anywhere else I have searched," he repeated, still looking around as if I were not present.

Not receiving an answer, I said, "the object must have been small for an animal to carry it off."

"Small, yes, but large in what it does accomplish." He again became silent, then said, "not an animal, then perhaps a human being?" He seemed to be talking more to himself.

"A human being? There were three men who passed here not very long ago. I believe they were making their way back to the circus being held in a field not far away," I replied.

Looking at me, I noticed his large nose and old eyes. "Three men, you say?"

"Yes sir, I have seen them a few days ago in the village handing out circus leaflets. They passed me earlier as I walked by the river. They were partly dressed as clowns."

"Clowns?" you say, "and they would have walked across this field?"

"Yes sir, this is the path most people use when making their way towards the village of Christchurch."

7

"Good Missy, do I implore you to help me in my distress, there appears to no-one else I might turn. Assist me if you will. I must, at all costs, retrieve that which is most precious to me and which is now missing. What reward can I offer you for your assistance? What doth you desire? It is in my power as Abbott of my priory to reward you if you shall so assist me to regain that most precious item. I am to place it within a certain church before a time does expire. Then if not done, thereafter all shall become darkness."

Seeing my hesitation, he paused as he seemed to gaze around for somewhere to rest himself. Noticing an old tree stump, he shuffled towards it, sitting down and becoming silent for a moment, then saying, "may I please take a little more of your time that I may explain my position and you will understand my predicament although my tale may cause you some confusion."

Again I waited for him to continue also wondering about the places I had thought to visit.

"Many centuries ago, the great gods of the ancient world of the Mediterranean vied with each other as to who would take control of a sacred article, placed upon the high altar in the temple dedicated to the God Zarmerious, the God of knowledge and enlightenment." He paused as if trying to breath normally. "The sacred Item, placed near to the statue of the God had many properties the ancient people could not explain, but could use. A structure with dials, allowing the temple priests to work out the times of the tides, the next eclipse and when famine would strike the community. The barbarians, then attacking and overrunning the ancient lands of Greece and attacking the town, knew of the sacred relic and it's strange magical properties. They were eager to take it and place it upon an altar in their own temple. Soon they would attack and sack the temple of the God Zarmerious."

"What happened?" I asked, then wondering if I should have interrupted the old man.

"Knowing of the attack and not wishing the sacred item to be used in worship in any other temple, the God Zarmerious, from the heavens above, thrust down great bolts of lightning upon the attacking army, thus delaying their progress through the embattled town and allowing the religious priests of the temple the time necessary to save it. Entrusting it to a distant religious order for safety, it has been handed down through the centuries to the Lord Abbots of the 'Order of Zarmerious' with it's presence known only to the senior leaders within the order. The order existed in an ancient religious monastery on the banks of the River Hamble. It remained there until the Monastery was destroyed on the orders of the King of England. Since that time, it has been protected in great secrecy in religious places in the deepest and darkest Hampshire forest, once a favourite of kings for hunting."

"Are you referring to the 'New Forest?" I asked.

Without answering my question directly, he continued, "I was attempting to make my way to Christchurch Priory where the monks were due this last night to give me food and shelter. Within an agreed period was I to deliver my precious package to an ancient village church, where my successor would take from my shoulders the responsibility I have these many decades endured. I shall then rest my weary body as I am now of advanced years, relieved at having transferred the responsibilities to another more able." Turning to look up at me, he continued, "the problem, young lady, is there are those who would wish the relic for themselves for the power it can give them. There is the evil wicked Cretonious. He was in the past a wizard, but also became an Abbott of a nearby priory. Learning of the magical powers of the sacred relic when such knowledge was forbidden, he tried in vain to steal it causing serious injury to a senior monk guarding the relic. His punishment reduced him to a lower rank and with less authority over others in that community. As a past wizard, he still posses some of the power he once enjoyed. He does still threaten others, trying to scare those he does address. I now ask you to assist me to find and recover this most important relic that it may continue to serve those of good intent."

"I would like to help you find your relic,"I said, but then asked, "how could I possible help you? I am a schoolgirl and only seeking a summer job during the holidays, this being the first day of the holidays."

He again paused as if what I had said and his explaining his problem had caused him to become more breathless. He continued slowly, "the item doth inform the position of the stars and eclipse. It also has properties not understood by man that allow the guardian access to great powers. I have exercised a few of those powers, allowing me to help those most in need, but times are now changing. Great changes are occurring in the universe above and I must now hand over the power that this item does bestow on the holder, as only a younger stronger human being shall have the strength to take over the responsibility once allowed me. Another shall grow in their responsibility as I once did, but that person is unknown to me and I to that person. My final mission is to safely leave the ancient item in the safety of a church known only to myself and one other."

Pausing again as if he were alone, he then, after a short pause continued, "I hope I have made you aware of how important I must recover the item and with all speed."

"I only know of the three men I passed a short while ago," I said, trying to be helpful. "The ones working for the circus being held during the summer season on the recreation ground. They have waited for the storm to pass before erecting their big top which I now believe they are now doing."

"I am aware of your intention to travel hoping to see a rare bird upon these marshes and then to journey to Mudeford quay for an inspection of a new contraption. May you not instead assist me in a journey for which is most important to all, as the road I travel is finally coming to an end, with my strength failing?"

"A journey?" I started to say, wondering how he knew of my plans for visiting both the marsh and the quay during the morning.

"My life's journey will end in tragedy for many of good heart, if the relic is finally to be delivered into the hands of he who would use it to enrich his own power and thus deny those riches to others less fortunate. Will you not consider to assist me?"

"I am not sure about, what I mean is I would like to help," again I hesitated, "do you mean for me to find those men and ask about your relic?"

"More than that, to assist me in my quest by assisting in the work of this circus of which you speak?"

"The circus probably already has all the assistance it needs, but it would be nice to have a summer holiday job working in a circus, meeting all those interesting people and animals, especially looking after the Shetland ponies," I replied. "Of course, even if I was offered the job, I could only do it during the holidays. I will be going back to school when that ends."

"Think about the fun no further, my power will assist you and you shall not be missed by your family. If you are successful and return the sacred relic to me, I will use it to adjust the time you are away. Fear not, but I must emphasize the item is fragile and villains might damage it for the small number of jewels is does contain."

"I could go to the circus and ask if they need any help during the season while the circus is in Christchurch or any local town," I suggested, but I was interrupted.

"No need, no need," the old man said. "Close now your eyes and imagine you are entering the circus tent as the crowds come to be seated and the children especially looking forward to the event. You shall not allow any person to know you seek the relic. The wicked wizard Cretonious will appear only if he is suspicious or thinks you have discovered it. I will be with you and will have knowledge if that time comes. Go now, my age calls for me to further continue my rest before I continue my journey to meet the monks at the Priory."

"Sir, there are no longer any monks in Christchurch Priory, the order was closed many centuries ago. Only the church building remains," I replied.

"Yes, yes, I already know that which you wish to tell me. The monks do still continue their work, although smaller in number, but from lodgings close to the Priory and unseen by all others. They pray still in the priory church, but after the tower clock has chimed the midnight hour, when all persons in the town are asleep in their beds and the graveyard silent. Go now, I must rest, but will return when I will know my assistance is required."

As I watched the old man, bending low, make his way slowly towards the shelter of a tree, he turned and called back to me, "fear not the task you are to undertake."

Hesitating, I wondered what I should do. Still unsure I began walking across the field thinking about all the old man had told me and what he was asking me to do. Stopping after a short while and looking around, I wondered if I was walking along the right path as the scenery seemed different from when I had walked along the path earlier. I seemed to be in front of and just about to walk into a very large tent, although I do believe tents as big as the one before me are called marquees. Looking up, I don't think I have ever seen a marquee so high or so large.

The Abbott will stay in Christchurch Priory.

Walking nervously into the marquee, I became suddenly aware of the number of people around me, all busily doing things. Many were walking around, others talking to other people and others unpacking large boxes and arranging chairs and other furniture. Ropes were being used to lift beams and other items high above me. In what seemed a mass of people doing a great number of things, I could only stand and stare, wondering how so many people knew what they needed to do to make a circus ready for a performance. Suddenly a small man with long red hair rushed past me. "Don't just stand there, help to get the trapeze equipment upto the roof of the marquee," he called out as he continued on his way.

Chapter Two

The circus, three conjurers, two Richards,

Priory house and a strange mirror.

"Miss Jemima, isn't it?" called out a rather rotund lady as she emerged from the crowd of busy circus entertainers and workers all seeming to be doing something and all in a great hurry to do whatever it was they were doing. "Of course it is, it must be. I knew it was you at once and that you are due to join us today so I naturally came to look for you. So nice to see you here. I am Mrs Hibbard and I like to look after the young people helping us run this circus as we travel the various towns and villages in Dorset," she said as she put her hand on my shoulder, leading me further into the tent. "How long have you been with us? Oh silly me, you have only just joined us, haven't you. Has the ringmaster seen you and already given you any tasks to do, because if he has I shall be giving him a talking to and he knows what that will mean?"

"Er no," I replied, looking at this strange lady and the very old fashioned clothes she wore. I noticed first the yellow apron she was wearing over a dark blue dress and the many pockets on the front of the apron, then her hair concealed under a cotton cap."

"That is as it should be," she continued. "If I have told him once, I have told him many times, he is not supposed to give out any circus tasks to any young people without first asking me. I am in charge of the welfare of the young ladies and young gentlemen who assist us in this circus. He really is an old duffer. Despite my telling him, he will still keep

14

interfering in my side of the day to day circus activities. Such daily tasks should only be offered to our younger assistants through me, don't you agree? I mean, that is what I am here for or why else am I here? Now what sort of circus tasks would you imagine you would like to do? There are a number of things we need doing each day. Let me see, I have a list here somewhere or did I leave it where I recently was. Just give me a minute and I will remember where I recently was before I came to meet you."

"Meet me?" I asked. "Thank you for coming to meet me, but how did you know I would be coming to the big tent, I suppose I should say, marquee, when I did and how could you know my name?"

"An elderly man in a long coat with a hood over most of his head suddenly appeared before me just a short while ago and told me you were just approaching the entrance to our marquee and would be the ideal person to work with our animals, I also believe he mentioned our Shetland ponies."

"An old man?" I began to say, but the lady was more intent on searching the many pockets on the front of her apron than listening to what I was saying.

Pulling out a large red handkerchief she continued. "I can be a little forgetful sometimes." she confessed. "Ah, now here we are." Looking at the piece of paper in her hand, she said, "no sorry, that was the list of things I was supposed to do last week. When will I ever get time to do all the things I am supposed to do, but have never managed to get around to doing most of them? Things change so quickly in a circus from day to day. First things first, that is what my late husband, Mr Hibbard always use to say. "If in doubt Mrs hibbard," he would say, "always put first things first and then second things must come second."

Pausing as she again searched through her many pockets, pulling out another large handkerchief, she continued, "I always thought that was a marvellous piece of advice and so clever, don't you think? Although, between the two of us, I am not sure I really understood what it meant. Still, Mr Hibbard, I think, was always pleased when I listened to him saying it. Now, where can we find you to stay while you are with us? Why of course, there is Miss Grager, she is in a wheelchair at present. A lovely girl, I am sure she will be happy to have someone nearer her own age to talk to and share her caravan. She did tell me recently she was sometimes a little lonely, being by herself in her caravan."

Searching again her many apron pockets, she read from a piece of paper and continued, "your name is at the very top of my list of young people joining us today, which is very strange because a number of younger people have asked me during the week if they could help out at the circus for the holiday season. I asked each one to come this morning, but you are the only person to have arrived. Now, as you are the only one on my list, you do have a pick of the tasks we need doing while you are with us. The elderly gentleman did say you would be with us during your summer holiday. The people rushing around you see now are all busy erecting the marquee and it's supports, ready for tomorrow's performances. Can't have it come crashing down on the audience, can we?"

"You had me on your list of those who would be joining the circus today?" I again asked.

"At the very top of my list as I said," she replied. "You decided to choose us instead of continuing your journey to see that rare bird of the marsh, which I do believe would have flown away before you had a chance to see it. Now I am still wondering which type of task you would be happiest doing while you are with us."

"I had a friend who looked after the ponies at stables not far from where I live and she was happy doing that," I suggested, hoping I could

16

help in looking after any of the smaller animals.

"Animals," you say and the elderly gentleman did mention Shetland ponies. That would be very useful, as I have only just learned that one of the young ladies looking after our animals had to leave us to look after a family member. I shall take you see Miss Grager and away from the noise and bustle in the marquee and take you to a much quieter area where we look after and feed the animals."

With that she turned and began pushing her way through the throng of people, beckoning me with her hand to follow her and stay close as possible. Leading me finally towards the rear of the marquee, we emerged into a quieter area where I noticed a number of caravans with open sides and areas roped off where small ponies were grazing. Walking past these, we entered a smaller tent where a girl slightly older than myself was sitting in a wheelchair and reading a book nestled on her lap. Seeing us, she looked up and smiled.

"This is Miss Grager, who I am sure, will be happy for you to call her by her name, Carrie-Ann."

Smiling the girl held out her hand to me, "of course, Carrie-Ann."

"Jemima," I said looking down at her in her wheelchair and gently holding her hand.

"Well now, I shall leave you two to get acquainted. Miss Jemima would prefer to help in some way to look after the smaller animals, perhaps the Shetland ponies." Leaving the tent, she called back to me, "I shall return when I have a moment and see how you are getting on. Remember, if the ringmaster should see you and try to give another task, you should find me or tell him politely, you already have a task which will take up much of your days while you are with us. Goodbye."

There was a short silence before either of us spoke.

"I have your bed all made up and ready," she said.

"My bed?" I replied, wondering what she meant.

"Yes," she replied, "A tall man came into my caravan and said it had been arranged you would be helping out for the summer season and as we are of similar age, I might like to allow you to stay in my caravan. I was quite surprised as I had never seen him before. I did agree, because being in a wheelchair, I am often lonely for company in the evenings and he did say some very nice things about you."

"Thank you for allowing me to share your caravan," I said, but then asked, "I wonder how the man knew I would be joining the circus today. I only thought about it myself a short time ago."

"A strange man, I thought," she added. "He was so tall he had to bend down to come into my caravan. I did notice his long cloak and the many buttons on the front. I wondered how long it takes him to button them each time. I could only see a small part of his face as his hood covered much of his head, so I probably would not know him if he returned except by his cloak and hood. Still, you are here now so that is all settled. You will stay with me and tomorrow morning, I can introduce to our Shetland ponies and tell you about how to feed them and how to exercise them."

With that she showed me the bed I was to use and offered to show me around the circus, but being in a wheelchair, she thought it might be better to wait until early tomorrow morning as she had a task to carry out during the afternoon.

"And you also have a funfair," I noted.

"Oh yes, always very popular and sometimes busier than the circus performances," was the reply. "If you would like to wander around by yourself to explore what you can and return in about an hour, I can take you to our canteen where we have our meals."

Thanking her, I put my coat on the bed I was to use and made my way to the door. Making my way back towards the circus marquee, I was now able to see how very high it was and was about to go in, but with all the activity inside, thought instead I would explore some of the large scenery and props gathered together in a nearby tent, which I assumed, would be used by the various performers.

"Who you be then?" a voice called over to me. "Don't ever remember seeing you before. You be part of the new tightrope act, are you, heard there was a new girl coming?"

Looking around I was both surprised and glad to see one of the three men I had seen earlier in the morning, whilst walking across Stanpit Recreation ground.

"Hello," I said, wanting to ask about the relic the old man had lost, but remembering the old man saying I should be careful in letting no-one know of my task in trying to recover the item.

"You new here?" he asked. "Ain't never seen you before," he again asked.

Seizing the opportunity, I replied, "yes, you have seen me before, but you may not have noticed me. This morning, just for a short time. I walked past you and two others. We passed each other across the recreation ground."

"Oh yes, coming from Mudeford Quay, we were. Trying to catch something, ended up instead catching nothing except perhaps a cold with all that rain and wind. Lasted till early this morning the rain did, lucky the marquee is not damaged."

"You were carrying a small parcel. I think that is what I noticed about you," I added, hoping the man would say something helpful and not wonder why I had mentioned the parcel.

"Small parcel?" he asked, scratching his head. "Small parcel, small parcel," he repeated. Then becoming silent, exclaimed, "oh yes, a small parcel. Found it we did on the grass. Blown away from somewhere nearby probably. Don't know where though. Didn't realise until I picked it up, how warm it was, like it was alive."

Waiting for him to say more, I was disappointed at his silence. Eventually, he added, "didn't seem no good. Might even be dangerous, could even explode and that be the end of us and us being the best clowns in the business."

"Oh," I said, waiting and hoping he would say more.

"Still, that be Madame Shavtof's business. Said it was an ancient relic, she did, and thought it might turn out to do lots of horrible things to anyone who did horrible things to it. So I said to her, I said, what sort of horrible things do you mean? And so she says to me, she says, horrible things like breaking it or taking bits out of it, so I says to my fellow clowns, I said, let's dump it, first chance we get. That's what I told them."

"What did you do?" I asked, hoping not to be asked, why my interest in the object.

"Didn't know the best thing to do, we didn't. Puts it on our dressing table we did, then we goes out to help with tidying up the stuff in the circus after last night's storm, when we returned later, it be gone. When the monkey man came and asked if anyone had seen his monkey, we find out the monkey had got into our dressing room and taken it. Took it upto the highest point of the circus marquee, he did, so we couldn't get it back again, not that we really wanted to. The monkey man coaxed him finally, so the thing is still up there I suppose. Of course, if Madame Shavtof had told us it be of value, then it be a different story. Then we three be interested in it and do try to find it again. Perhaps even open our own circus, just us three. Anyway if you be part of the new tightrope act, you could get it down."

"No, I will be looking after some of the animals," I replied.

"William, that's my mate," he said, "just as well if it stays up there, but then we don't want it falling down on someone's head, do we?" Stopping and thinking, he looked at me and asked, "who did you say you are and what you do here?"

"My name is Jemima Jones and I am here for the summer holidays to help look after the young animals," I again replied.

"That be nice, but make sure you see our act, best part of the circus, we be, best part of the circus. "There's me Albert, that be my name. I'm the tall one, then there be Bertrum, he be the short one, then there be Daniel, he be the one in the middle. Not too tall nor too small either, he always tells us."

"Pleased to know you," I answered, wondering how I could make an excuse to continue exploring the circus, but he interrupted me.

"Best be on my way now, you be sure to the see the act we three have prepared for the crowds. Fills the marquee with laughter that reaches clear upto the very top of the marquee, it does," as he turned and wandered off.

Watching him go, I turned around to continue my journey, only to find two strange looking men just behind me and each smiling up at me. Each had their hair cut so a fringe almost covered their eyes and each were short in height as they only came upto my waist.

"Bet you be thinking, there's two strange men standing just behind you and smiling at you. Did you think the young lady is thinking the same thing, did you, brother Richard?"

"Indeed I did, brother Richard, indeed I did. Shall we introduce ourselves to the young lady, brother Richard, do you think this might be the right time to introduce ourselves?"

"Now that you mention it, brother Richard, I think your suggestion to introduce ourselves to this young lady is apt."

"Apt?" replied the second person. "Yes, considering the circumstances, I believe the word 'apt' to be the correct word to be used on this occasion."

"Do you really, brother Richard, sometimes I think you are so clever."

"If you think I must be clever, then you also must be clever because we are twins."

As the two persons seemed to be talking to each other and forgotten about me, I said, "I am just starting helping with the small animals for the summer season and my name is Jemima, Jemima Jones."

"Well," said one, "now isn't that a very nice name, don't you agree brother Richard?"

"Agree?" asked the other man. "I am usually in agreement with you, but what specifically do you want me to agree about?"

"The young lady's name of course, brother Richard. I was just asking if you agree with me the young lady has a very nice name."

"Nice name? Oh yes, very nice name, very nice name. I do not believe I have heard of a nicer name this whole morning. Would you not agree, brother Richard?"

"Perfect agreement, brother Richard, perfect agreement."

"I thank you for both being in agreement about my name," I interrupted. "Perhaps you could tell me your names."

"Our names? Of course, brother Richard, we have been very rude and still have not introduced ourselves, we were going to do that, weren't we. We must have forgotten. The young lady would like to know our names."

"Then I do believe brother Richard, this would be a good time and probably the best time, to let the young lady know our names."

Turning to me, one man smiled and asked, "are you ready? My name is Richard and I am this other person's twin." The other man smiled at me and said, "my name is Richard and I am also this other person's twin, there are just the two of us and that is why we are twins."

Puzzled, I remained silent, then said, "surely if you are both named Richard, that must be confusing for when people wish to talk to either one of you."

"Now that is exactly what our dear mother said, confusion, that was the very word she used. She really did wish to avoid confusion. The world is confusing enough she said, so when thinking of which names to give us, as she later explained to us, if she called us by two different names, she would be always confused trying to remember the two different names as we are and always have been, twins. One name would be far easier to remember, she thought and so less confusing, so we now both have the same name. Wasn't that very clever of our dear mother to think that way an avoid all that confusion?"

"Very clever of our dear mother," repeated the other man, then continued, "actually, our dear departed mother did call my brother here Richard One and I became Richard Two. There was however, always the argument as to who should be called Richard One because our dear mother could not be sure who was the first born and therefore who should be called Richard One as we both looked alike as we still do. We later both decided to drop the formality of a formal name and we each became just 'Richard'. I am sure you will agree this was a very sensible thing to do."

"Yes," interrupted the other Richard, "we do both like to do sensible things, sometimes on formal occasions we do like to be formal, so I become Richard One on weekdays."

"And on those occasions, I become Richard One on Weekends," added the other person.

Confused, I thought it best to change the subject. "I was told a monkey had taken an item upto the ropes used by the trapeze artists and left it there."

"Oh no. That is old news. We know the latest news, don't we brother Richard?"

"Indeed we do, indeed we do, brother Richard. Are you going to tell the young lady the latest news?"

"The latest news?" I asked.

"Just a short time ago, we both saw the monkey climb upto the top of the marquee a second time on those rope things and we both watched it come down again with that item you referred to, did we not, brother Richard?"

"Indeed we did, brother Richard, indeed we did," was the reply.

"There, so what do you think of that latest news?" one Richard asked. "We both saw the monkey climb down with the object, but then it ran off, although where we don't know," the other Richard added.

"Could be anywhere, could be anywhere, but he has a cage. You could ask the monkey keeper if you think the item is worth the trouble of asking," the first Richard said. "You could ask the monkey keeper," he repeated as I said nothing.

Thanking them, I politely turned and mentioned how I was trying to find my way around the circus and the funfair as I had only just joined the circus.

"Don't get lost. When you have been here as long as we have, we must know all the ways to go by now," called out one Richard as they began to walk away.

"Don't get lost," I heard the other Richard call out. Then a little later, he continued, "shouldn't we be going in that direction?"

"No, no. I am sure we should be going in this other direction," suggested the other Richard.

"Dear oh dear, there are so many ways to go these days. It is all so confusing, not a bit like the good old days" one called out.

"So, so confusing," the other Richard called out.

Lunch in the circus canteen was interesting as many performers were wearing their circus costumes as they had spent some of the morning rehearsing their acts and were intending to continue during the afternoon.

It was only a short while after we had finished lunch that Carrie-Ann mentioned she had a meeting during the afternoon at Priory House in Christchurch and as it was not very far away, she wondered if I should like to accompany her.

Priory House, Christchurch.

"The house is very old and is situated just behind Christchurch Priory. I can make the way there in the wheelchair without any problem. I am arranging a merry-go-round for the children during the next few days for the Priory church staff and volunteers," she explained. "If you accompany me, we can make the arrangements together."

I had often visited Christchurch Priory, but was unfamiliar with Priory House

"Because it is built behind the Priory," she said, "many people do not know of it because they do not usually visit that side of the Priory."

Saying how much I would like to opportunity to accompany her, I was glad of the invitation. Off we set from the recreation ground, then along the path adjoining a stream until we reached Bridge Street. From there we made our way the short distance into Christchurch village, turning towards the Priory. Walking through the cemetery, I was led past the main door and towards the far side of the church. There, we made our way across a large lawn and towards Priory House, which I had seen before, but had taken little notice as it had always been partly hidden, due to where it was.

"This lawn is where we are thinking of siting the merry-go-round," Carrie-Ann whispered to me. "It is large enough for the merry-go-round and still allows plenty of room for the visitors, but it is on a slope, so we must first fix that," she added.

Looking up at the very impressive front of the house, I mentioned how I had never taken much notice of the house before.

"It is very historic," replied Carrie-Ann. "While I am making the arrangements and meeting some of the people, which might take some time, I will ask if you can look around the house as I believe much of it is unoccupied."

A short while later after she had left me, I heard a very deep voice behind me say, "Miss, please to follow me." Turning, I noticed a tall elderly man, bent almost double, approaching me and pointing towards the house. Dressed in a long black coat with a large bunch of keys in his hand, he added, "this way if you please. The main entrance is just a short walk this way." Making our way towards the entrance and it's impressive door, he fiddled with his keys in the lock as he struggled to find the correct one. "I will lock you in, when you are ready, ring the door bell and I will return to let you out," he said. "Must keep the house secure, can't have strangers just walking in, can we?"

Thanking him as he turned to go, he stopped to mention the rooms to be interesting but empty and the house very old. "There have been tales of ghosts haunting this house," he said in his deep gravel voice. "I think they originated many years ago when there were smugglers on the marshes and in this village. This house being so close to the marshes, the harbour and the old George Inn, where smugglers would meet to divide and hide their contraband."

Holding his hand to his mouth to stop a cough, he continued, "there are those who will tell you the tales were simply made up to scare away prying eyes so the smugglers could do their work without interruption." Coughing again, he tried to continue. "Those old tales have existed to this day. There was also the tale of the headless horseman who would ride his black horse across the marshes, scaring anyone who ventured out on the marshes at night, also keeping the revenue men away from the marshes." Turning, he locked the door behind me, then disappeared, I supposed around the side of the building.

Making my way into the main hall, I wondered slowly around the downstairs rooms, admiring the many views of the marshes from the windows. As the house was built on a hill, I could also see the mouth of the harbour and Hengistbury Head in the distance. Finding myself at the bottom of the main stairway, I climbed the bare wide oak stairs to the upper rooms on the first floor. One door on the landing did interest me. It was very large, very dark door and contained a number of carvings of strange faces. Most were of strange demon type figures and I thought, a little scary so I did wonder if I should enter the room. The door, being so heavy, was difficult for me to push open, there being no handle on the door, which I thought strange. Thinking I should instead explore another room, I had just taken a few steps towards another part of the corridor, but was astonished as the door suddenly swung open, making a loud noise as it banged back against the wall.

Hesitating and looking through the opening, I thought the room to be completely empty except for a very large mirror against the far wall. Surrounded with small wooden carvings similar to those on the door, there was something different about it, but I was not sure what. Walking hesitantly into the room and closer to the mirror, I stood looking into it. The first thing I noticed was my reflection did not appear. Gradually the colourless empty surface began to filled with a slow moving greyish colour that flowed down from the top of the mirror. As I placed my hand on the mirror, I realised the changing colours were behind the surface of the mirror. These was soon replaced with a dull yellow, until the whole of the mirror became a yellow colour. Fascinated, I watched as colour replaced colour. Each time the colours changed, they moved in a wavy fashion, moving this way and that without any regular pattern forming.

So puzzled was I at what I was seeing and what could be the cause of such a strange effect, I became a little nervous and felt I should step back and leave the room. However, the effects so dazzled me that I found myself unable to stop watching the changing colours and effects. Sometimes a colour would appear at the top of the mirror, which was so high the top almost reached upto the ceiling, then gradually the colour would float down behind the surface of the mirror, blending in with colours towards the bottom. Other colours would at the same time begin to float upwards.

Although fascinated, my eyes became a little blurred and my head dizzy as I continued watching the various changes of colour. Determined I should not watch anymore as my dizziness increased, I closed my eyes, turned and began to slowly make my way back towards the door.

I had not gone more than a few steps, when a voice called to me, causing me to immediately stand still and open my eyes. "Young lady, you will please turn and face me as my birthright demands," Turning again to face the mirror, I was shocked to see a man standing there. Unable to understand how he had appeared, I just stared at him and his strange clothes.

"You should bow before me and I will accept that," he said in the voice of an older man.

Quite not knowing what to say, I just looked at him. A medium sized man, quite plump and with hair that reached down to his shoulders. His clothes were a velvet colour and he wore, what I thought must be thin socks or stockings reaching upto his knees. I was startled and a little nervous as I then noticed he had a sword fastened to his wide belt.

"I repeat, you should bow to me. In my present circumstance, I believe that to be most appropriate due to my birth and present situation."

"Sir," I stammered, "how did you suddenly appear, there was no-one here a moment ago?"

"Appear? Nonsense, I am here in this house. This is my dwelling until I am again where my birthright is recognised by my countrymen and where I should be. Your name, young lady?"

"Sir, I am here with my friend who is presently," but then my voice became weaker and then I found I could make no sound. I could not think what else I could say even if I could speak.

"Why are you here, why do you interrupt my peace?" he asked in a stern voice. "This house is allowed to me and I will share it with no-one. No-one, you understand?" he said, his voice becoming louder.

Strolling to the window and seeming to look over towards the marshes, he said, more to himself than to me, "there is likely a storm before the darkness does descend this night."

"Sir, I am sorry to have disturb you," I said, finding my voice again. "I was asked if I would like to view the house as I was told it is unoccupied."

"And so it is, young lady, and so it is. I exist not here, but from there do I come," and he pointed towards the mirror.
Remaining silent and feeling I should leave the room, I thought of something to say as I made my way towards the door, but all I could think to say was, "my name is Miss Jemima Jones and."

"And you see before you the King of France," he said, interrupting me, placing one hand on his hip.

"The King of France," I repeated. Then taking a deep breath added, "Sir, I do not wish to appear rude, but I was not aware there is a King of France."

"The King of France you see before you. I am here but waiting, but for what? I have been waiting these long months and am still waiting." Turning to look at me with an angry expression on his face, he said, "for how much longer must I wait. Know you that?"

He was silent for a moment as he again turned to look out of the window and across the misty marshes.

"I am Louis Philippe, King of France," he announced, as if speaking to a large audience.

Slowly making my way towards the door, which I was disappointed to see was now closed, I had no choice but to turn and ask, "Sir, when were you, I mean, are you now the King of France?" thinking to humour him.

"When? When you ask." He became silent, then said, "my reign was after Napoleon the first, but before Napoleon the third."

"Napoleon the third,"I repeated. Then suddenly remembering a visit I had made to Farnborough in Hampshire to stay with a school friend, I burst out, "Sir, I have visited the tomb of Napoleon the Third, when I visited a friend in the town of Farnborough. I think it was two years ago."

"Napoleon the third buried in an English town and I am here in an English town awaiting my return, but for how much longer. Again I ask, for how much longer?"

He was silent for a short while then said, "go now, I must rest. Tell no-one you have seen me lest they disturb the peace I have found here."

Slowly he seemed to slide, rather than walk, towards the mirror. Seeing my chance, I turned and quickly made my way towards the door. As I came closer, wondering how I was going to open such a large door, it suddenly swung open, allowing me to quickly walk through. Once out into the corridor, I turned and was astonished to see the now smaller figure of the person seeming to float up and into the mirror. Stunned I watched as once into the mirror, the figure floated into the distance and then disappeared as the colours quickly returned and covered him. The large door, swung itself shut and I was left looking, face to face at the many carved faces surrounding the door. A few of the more grotesque seemed to be looking directly at me as if wanting me to go away.

It was a few minutes before I could think what I should do, so confused and nervous was I. There were many rooms I had not yet explored, but my only thought was to quickly make my way down the stairs and towards the front door. Standing there in the hall was the same tall man who opened the door for me, as if waiting for me.

"I did not think you would want to stay very long inside this house," he said as he held open the door, "no-one ever does, so instead of going very far away, I returned and waited for you."

Thanking him and walking quickly through the door, I spied Carrie-Ann in her wheelchair as she made her way across the lawn, perhaps wondering if I was ready to rejoin her.

"Hello," she called out. "I thought you might be ready to see the arrangements I have managed to make about the merry-go-round and where it will be positioned."

Thanking her and allowing myself a short time to calm down, I quietly asked her, "was there ever a king living in this house?"

"A king?" She stopped to think. "Oh yes, I think there is a plaque somewhere, I don't know if it is still there. It must have been about the time of the French Revolution. Louis Philippe was his name and he was the King of France. He lived in this house while he was in exile from his own country. I believed he returned when it was safe enough for him to go back to France. That was many, many years ago. If there is nothing more you wish to see, we can make our way back to the circus as I think I have dealt with all the details regarding the merry-go-round. I can explain to you when we are again in our caravan. It will be soon time for tea. Circus people tend to have it later and we call it high tea." Following her as she carefully guided her wheelchair between the many tourists, we made our way back along Bridge Street, along the path by the stream and finally to our caravan.

Chapter Three

Exploring Stanpit Marshes

and meeting three strangers.

Waking up early, probably due to my going to bed early, I decided as the daylight was creeping in through the small window above my bed, I would not disturb Carrie-Ann, but get myself ready for an early morning walk across the marshes. I was due to exercise two of the Shetland ponies on the marshes later during the morning, so the walk would give me the opportunity to see more of the marshes and where best to exercise the ponies.

With the recreation ground close to the marshes now deserted, this was my chance to explore as far as I dared go, with no-one to disturb me. Approaching the narrow entrance to the marshes, I was now close to the tall trees where yesterday I had seen the strange man who was so worried about the loss of his sacred relic. Wondering if I would see him again soon, I reminded myself of my promise to him to help find his religious Item, hoping it was still somewhere in the circus. Otherwise I was not sure how I would go about helping him find the relic.

Walking across muddy grass, I tried to avoid the shallow pools, rabbits darting quickly back into their warrens, undulating hills and the many streams flowing furiously across the marshes and out towards the harbour entrance. In the far distance and against the water's edge, I could make out the many horses roaming the marshes as they munched the grass, moving from one place to another. The recent storms meant having to jump the distance from one area of higher ground to another nearby area of higher ground. Beyond the horses and the few sandy areas close to the wide river Avon as it flowed out towards the small submerged islands, I could see the trees and bushes growing on the far side of the harbour, known as Hengistbury Head with it's historic iron age workings and past settlements.

Stanpit marsh and Hengistbury Head.

Looking again across the deserted landscape, I began to notice various breeds of birds wadding and feeding in the many pools. There was no sign of the rare bird I had hoped to see. I was surprised to see a large bird, I believe a buzzard, perched on the rail of a small upturned boat, now beached and slowly rotting away. Turning to look towards the distinctive tower of the Christchurch Priory, I wondered if the old man, managed to meet whoever it was he was trying to meet, after the recent nights' storm.

Looking back towards the part of the marshes reserved as a bird sanctuary, the large buzzard was now gone. In the same spot, however, I was very surprised to see a smallish man waving to me. Wondering why and how be came to be there, I immediately assumed he was having difficulty walking across the soggy ground as parts of the marsh were still considered too dangerous to walk on.

"Young lady," he called out. "A moment of your time, if you do please."

As he struggled to make his way across the many pools and soggy ground, I waited for him to come closer. Approaching me, I noticed and was puzzled by the clothes he wore. A man of middle age with the top of his head shaven, but with the rest of the hair untouched. He wore a long dark cloak buttoned up with black buttons and seeing him, I remembered the cloak worn by the elderly man I had spoken to previously. The hood attached to the man's cloak lay back across his shoulders. Supported by a long stick as he used it to guide himself across the soggy ground, he gradually made his way towards me.

"Young lady, so joyful am I that I have at last managed to find you here."

"Find me here, sir?" I replied.

"I mean, of course how joyful I am of finding another human being on this most desolate place, fit only for the animals I now see roaming and foraging for food that this miserable place does provide."

Unsure of what I should do and certainly of what I should say, I chose my words carefully. "I am surprised to see you here so early sir, as you see, the marshes are completely deserted of visitors so early this morning."

"Me thinks I would not see anyone on these marshes so early. The warmth of the sun has not yet time to better fit this wild and empty space for man or beast.

Saying nothing as I did not think it right for me to ask him about himself, I simply replied, "I am visiting the marshes as I shall be exercising a few circus ponies here later this morning and thought it best to find appropriate places to exercise them."

"Excellent and I know you will accomplish that task in a most commendable fashion. Now let me advise you of my task. I am expecting to meet in these parts another of my religious faith, for did he not traverse these dangerous marshes during that most turbulent recent storm. Last seen here was he and it would be the greatest comfort to me to learn he is both safe and well. May I politely enquire if you have been walking these marshes and the local areas at periods during these days. If so, might you then furnish me with such details as would allow me to find and visit him. I do of course wish him the best of health and am only interested in his safety. You may have seen an older gentleman, tall and wearing a cloak similar to the one I now wear?"

He became silent as I struggled to think. There was something about the way he was looking at me with his piecing eyes, as if trying to decide any answer I would give would be truthful. His manner and his voice also caused me to delay an answer as something about him made me feel a little uneasy.

"An older gentleman, tall and wearing a cloak similar to the one you now wear," I repeated, trying to think what else I should say.

"That is it, that is it," he repeated, coming ever closer to me and looking directly at me, causing me to step back apace.

Immediately I thought of the elderly gentleman asking me not to tell anyone of his presence. "I can't be sure," I answered. "There were so many people passing this way, especially after the storm," I paused, "and with the many people working in the circus now visiting the local area. I may have seen someone of that description, but I cannot be sure."

Stepping back and seeming disappointed, he said nothing, but continued to stare at me as if waiting for me to continue.

"You have not seen an elderly man of that description?" he again asked, still looking at me intently as if I was not telling the truth.

"You see before you, Friar Cretonious, one-time Abbott Cretonious. That is my title and that is my name," he announced. "I must also add, a member of a most important ancient religious order situated not here, but elsewhere and of a considerable distance away. Here shall I remain. Should you remember such a person of my description, you will of course find me most agreeable and with a most agreeable manner in which I shall reward you. Later, as the hours do this day pass, shall I take the opportunity to further enquire of others who do this place frequent and ask of them as I have asked of you. May I now thank you for the time you have allowed me, as I continue to search for my good colleague so I may be assured he is both safe and in good health."

"Good morning to you sir, as it must now be time for me to return to the circus and the tasks I must do this morning," I said, as with relief, I turned and made my way back across the old wooden bridge towards the recreation ground. I had not walked very far when the temptation to turn to see the stranger again was too great. As I turned, I was disappointed, but also relieved to see he was no longer anywhere on the marshes. What I did notice was the large buzzard almost where the person had been standing. I also noticed the long stick the stranger had used to support himself, was now lying on the ground and very close to the buzzard.

Feeling relieved to be nearing the caravan, I was happy to see Carrie-Ann sitting outside the caravan in her wheelchair and brushing the main and coat of a small brown pony.

"Morning," she called out, smiling as she noticed me approaching the caravan. "I do hope you enjoyed your early morning walk. Before my accident, I liked to enjoy walking wherever I happened to be and before the circus people were up and the main business of help running the circus needed to be attended to."

"I explored parts of the marshes," I replied. "The recent storm has made much of the ground quite soggy and there many new streams flowing across the marshes."

"This young pony is Paula who has been with the circus since she was born. Some ponies stand at about 42 inches high and Paula is nearly that. As you can see, she has a very stocky build and weighs about the same as two grown men, so she is well able to stand the conditions of the marshes and will enjoy a long walk whatever the conditions. Soggy or not, rain or sun, Paula will always look forward to her daily walk. Our other pony is Matilda, a Standard Shetland. Standards are larger, but Matilda will be seeing the circus vet today for a check-up. You will be feeding her with Paula later, but no walks for her until tomorrow. Paula, being a miniature Shetland pony, gives rides to young children from the age about three years. Children upto twelve years will ride on Matilda, being a Standard Shetland pony."

Walking forward and stroking the newly brushed coat of the young pony, I wondered about the accident Carrie-Ann had mentioned, but thought not to ask.

"Well now, that is enough for today," she said putting down the brush she had been using. "Now time for the all important first thing of the day, breakfast. After your early morning walk, you must be feeling quite hungry."

Agreeing, I followed her as she pattered the pony on the head and began to steer her wheelchair in the direction of the tent used as a canteen for circus staff and helpers.

Walking back alone after the meal, I found myself thinking about the old man and the strange person who had suddenly appeared on the marsh. One was an Abbott and the other was a friar who was once an Abbott. As I again found myself approaching the caravan, I began to feel excited about taking the pony for a walk. Waiting for my companion and patting the Shetland pony, I did not have to wait too long as Carrie-Ann and her wheelchair soon came into view.

"Some people," she said, "want to spend so long talking about the details of new acts they are thinking of introducing to the circus, I could not get away." Now nearing me, she continued, "there are two other circus members who would like to accompany you as you exercise Paula."

"Two others?" I asked, slightly disappointed that I would not be alone on my walk with Paula.

"Yes, two important members of the circus. There is Percy, unfortunately he is very talkative and Mickey. Mickey sometimes decides to run away when it suits him, but he always returns when he knows the canteen is open and again serving food, so if he decides to disappear, don't be too concerned. He will find his own way home."

Wondering who these two persons could be, I sat down again and waited for them to appear. After a short while, an old man emerged from a nearby tent with a parrot on one shoulder and a young monkey on his other shoulder.

"Here we are, all ready to enjoy a trip across the marshes," announced Carrie-Ann, much to my amazement as I looked at the two creatures.

"This is Mickey the monkey, who, as I said, might want to make his own way home if he gets bored with the walk and that is Percy, our parrot. Percy has been trained in an act, but generally causes such problems when she gets it wrong, the audience laughs more when she causes confusion than when she remembers what she should be doing."

"How will they travel?" I asked not sure about how I could control three circus animals whilst walking across the marshes.

"They will ride on Paula's back. They have done it many times before and Paula is used to them, she simply ignores them," was the welcome answer.

Still not sure, I unfastened the reins of the pony and gently pulled her towards me, surprised and satisfied that she meekly followed me.

"Get started, get started, no delay, no delay." the parrot squawked out loudly as it settled comfortably on the back of the pony. Jumping down from the man' shoulder, the monkey placed itself in front of the parrot, Immediately, the parrot squawked, "me front, me front."

"Those two always fight over who will be in front, I suppose to get the best views, just ignore them," advised Carrie-Ann.

Leading the pony gently on, I walked slowly forward, unsure how fast I should walk. After a few minutes, I found myself walking along at a pace I would normally walk and looking down, noticed the two sitting on the pony's back seeming content. Making my way through the grounds and tents, I finally guided the pony across the large recreation ground towards the start of the marshes.

"Faster, faster," squawked the impatient parrot. "Too slow, too slow," it continued.

However the various streams and ditches made it difficult for me to walk any faster so I had no choice but to continue as I was. Looking down at the donkey, I noticed the monkey was now in front of the parrot. Walking close to the end of the line of tall trees separating the marshes from the recreation ground, I looked up and was surprised and alarmed to see the figure of the same strange man, who had earlier appeared on the deserted marshes, to be sitting on a branch in the upper part of the tallest tree. Almost hidden by the leafy branches surrounding him, I was sure it was him. His dark coat almost hid him as did the many branches surrounding him. Guiding the pony further away from the trees so I could better see him, I walked through a nearby hedge onto a narrow pathway, hoping to get a better look. At first I could not see him as another branch hid him, then as I walked a little further on, I was again surprised and astonished to see a large buzzard was now perched on the branch I had thought I had seen the strange man.

Quickly looking across at the many branches, I searched for a further sighting of the man, but he had completely disappeared. I was sure I had seen him, but wondered how he could be so high in the tree without any means of climbing to that height.

I was now approaching the marshes so had to be careful where I led the pony. Looking back, having gone a short distance, I could now see the rear of the line of trees, but quickly searching, I was now not sure which tree I thought I had seen the strange figure. Lower down on another branch, I did see again the large buzzard and wondered if there was more than one.

At that moment, the parrot started squawking loudly, "nasty bird, nasty bird," and flew away into a group of dense bushes, as if worried of being attacked by the larger bird.

Thinking it might return soon, I decided the best thing to do would be to continue the journey towards the far end of the marsh, carefully crossing over the many streams and deep holes left by the many rabbits. Once there, I could continue the walk and return using another path running alongside the river Avon. After about half an hour, I finally reached the small sandy beach where the marsh met the outgoing river Avon and Stour combined. A number of swans, glided past being carried along by the fast flowing waters past submerged islands and towards the harbour entrance. As two of the group, probably curious, approached quite close to the beach. Mickey the monkey, seeing them, immediately jumped down from the pony's back, sprinted across the sand and leapt up onto the back of the nearest swan. Immediately the swan turned, bending it's neck, tried to push the monkey off it's back. As the monkey managed to avoid the swinging neck, the swan ruffled it's wings seeming to dislodge the monkey. With the monkey still on it's back, the swan swam away from the beach and towards the middle of the river, joining the group.

Seeing this, the parrot which had returned to sit on the pony's back, which I had not noticed, called out, "big fun, big fun," and immediately flew up and onto the back of the second swan, which quickly swam off to also join the group of swans.

Concerned and wondering what I should do, it seemed there was nothing I could do. I started out with two animals and one bird and I might now have return with just one animal to the circus. Looking around, I could see no-one to help me, but then what could anyone do, I wondered? There was nothing for me to do, but wait and hope at least the parrot would fly back to me, or perhaps make it's way back to the circus. Not knowing if monkeys can swim, I became concerned what I would say to Carrie-Ann on my return.

It was some minutes later, when looking across the bay and into the distance, I thought I could see a bird flying towards me. As it drew closer, it's colour told me it was parrot. Flying over my head several times as if to tell me it had returned, it then settled itself down on the back of the pony. At least the parrot had returned, now my concern was about the monkey. Deciding to wait for a further short time, I was so surprised, when the monkey suddenly emerged from under the water a short distance from the beach and swam awkwardly towards me. Reaching the beach, it ran across the narrow stretch of sand, leapt up onto the back of the pony, shook itself, scratched himself with a hind leg and settled down. Both then looked up at me as if waiting for me to continue the journey.

Continuing on with great relief, I made my way alongside the path close to the river and in the direction of Christchurch. Looking ahead, I noticed a large number of horses settled across the path, visitors would normally take. Some were lazily feeding while others lay on the grass asleep or just resting. All, however were blocking the path and were unlikely to move until they decided they wanted to move. Looking around I spied another newer path further inland that other visitors were probably already using, although none were in sight. Giving a gently pull on the rope to guide the pony to follow me, I trundled on.

I had not gone very far along the path when two men suddenly appeared from behind nearby bushes, with one raising his hand, preventing me from going any further.

Both were smiling, so I hoped them to be friendly. One was quite tall and thin and I instantly noticed the large square black hat which covered all of his head and some of his face. The other man, being much smaller and quite round, wore an old red cloth around his head, which was knotted at the back with the rest falling down his back. Both wore clothes, I thought, were quite old and needing several repairs. The taller of the two, with his tall hat making him look much taller, rested on a walking stick as if it was holding him up. The smaller of the two sat down on an upturned wooden box and stared up at me, still smiling.

"Young Missy, would you be wanting to use our path to get to wherever it is you wish to travel?" asked the taller of the two.

Now slightly nervous due to his tone, I wondered who these two men might be as I had never seen them before on the marshes. I replied, "like others before me, I cannot use the other paths as the horses are blocking my way and will probably be there for some time."

"So they are, so they are," he repeated. "Well now, it's a fine decision you have made to take this path, recently fashioned by my dear friend sitting there and myself. Indeed other travellers and walkers have made the same decision knowing it to be the right decision. Have they not, young Walter?" he asked the man sitting down.

"Tis right what you've just told the young lady, boss," the shorter man replied, "tis right enough."

"Then what did I just say?" the taller man asked.

"You were telling the young lady, er," the smaller man stopped, started scratching his head as if trying to remember what had been said.

"Will you be listening now," instructed the taller man. "I was just telling this young lady that other visitors to these marshes have made a fine decision to also use this path, so they have."

"Indeed you did, yes, now I come to think about the matter, that is what I believe you did tell the young lady, boss." The man seemed relieved.

"It is like this miss," continued the taller man, his hat waving about as he moved his head to speak. "We are travellers like yourself and have these past few days been busy making this path for those who would prefer to find themselves in areas of these marshes, they might not otherwise visit. Is that not right, young Walter?"

There being no reply from the man sitting on the upturned box, the taller man, shouted, "I said, was that not right, young Walter. Did you not follow what I was saying to the young lady?"

Stuttering, the man replied, "that was not right, that is what you told the young lady, I heard you say that, so I did, yes boss."

"Now that we are both in agreement, I should like to continue what I was about to mention to the young lady." Turning his attention to me, he continued, "we feel it only fair, as we have toiled for several hours to make this path through these bushes fit for decent folks that they may travel on their way safe and sound and in the knowledge that the moment they take our path, they are assured of a safe and satisfying journey and therefore free from brambles and stinging nettles. Do you agree with that, young Walter?" he again asked.

"What was that you asked, boss?" was the reply from the man sitting down. "Was it me you were addressing or was it the young lady here?" He seemed to be about to get up, but then decided instead to remain where he was. "I was following some of what you told the young lady, but then I became a little confused, so I did."

"I was addressing the young lady and was about to mention to the young lady that we feel obliged to ask for a small donation by way of a thank you, for creating this path through these many bushes due to the toil and effort made."

"A small donation?" I replied. "Surely paths over all these marshes are free for anyone to walk."

"Well yes, that is indeed the present situation. You are free to travel anywhere on these marshes, as are all those who should desire to do so. Is that not right, young Walter?"

"Is indeed the present situation, boss," the man on the box repeated, then added, "what was the next bit you said?"

"I said, in effect, there would be no charge for the young lady whatsoever. Indeed a small gift would be simply for the three animals that do now accompany her." Then addressing me, he said, "had you been walking alone along our path, the one we took so much trouble to create, why then of course there would be no charge." Then addressing again his friend, he asked, "would you be agreeing with me on that, young Walter?" he called down to the other man.

"It's agreeing I am with everything you are telling the young lady and very politely too, boss," was the reply.

Pausing, then looking at me, the taller man continued, "thinking carefully about the matter concerning these three animals. As there are horses grazing on the marshes and you have with you, what I perceive to be a very small horse, then the two of us would only ask for a contribution for the other two animals. Is that fair and proper, young Walter?" he asked.

"Fair and proper, fair and proper, it be, boss," repeated the other man.

Suddenly a rabbit emerged from under a bush and darted across the clearing, running towards a clump of thistles. Seeing it, the monkey jumped down and chased after it.

"Well now, would you look at that commotion," stated the man sitting on his box. "First there were two, now there is now only one animal left for which you can ask a small contribution."

"Well now, a small contribution for the one animal left, would be very welcome," continued the taller man.

"But I have come to be thinking on the matter and it does not seem right, boss," interrupted the smaller man.

"And why would it not be right?" questioned the taller man, seeming to become irritated with his friend.

"Well, the parrot a bird and a bird is not an animal," was the answer.

At that moment, the parrot seeing birds flying between the branches of trees in the distance, suddenly flapped his wings, muttering 'big fun, big fun' and flew towards the trees.

Looking after the departing parrot, the man sitting on his upturned box said, "it's me here thinking again to myself. With two animals and one bird gone, we have nothing left to charge the young lady for, boss. Would that be right thinking, would it?"

The taller man said nothing as if in thought, but then took off his very tall hat and bowing low, waved it in front of me, indicating I was free to pass. Managing to stand up again and replacing his hat, he murmured, "my deepest sympathy, young lady on the loss of your animals, please continue to use our path without any contribution."

Thanking the two of them, I pulled the pony gently forward. Having travelled a short distance across the marsh and beyond the trees, I was pleased when the monkey, sitting in a stone, suddenly appeared. As I came closer, it quickly leapt up onto the pony's back and settled itself down. Walking a short distance further, the parrot emerged from the trees, flew overhead several times, then also settled itself on the pony, wedging itself in front of the monkey. Walking on a few minutes, I looked down to see the monkey had manged to edge itself past the parrot and was now sitting content in front of the parrot.

"Everything alright, were there any problems on your first walk with our circus animals?" asked Carrie-Ann, as I entered the main circus marquee.

Looking at the monkey and parrot, I found myself answering, "no trouble at all, a very interesting walk."

Later, having rested, I wondered about Carrie-Ann. How long had she been with the circus and what was the reason for her being in a wheelchair. I thought it best to wait as she might provide me with details of her life as we became better acquainted.

"Time for an early lunch," she called out as she wheeled herself upto the front of the caravan. Letting her lead the way, I was content to follow and look around at the many performers either rehearsing their acts or moving their props around to where they wanted them.

Chapter Four

The marionettes, Priory House, the mirrors.
Priory church and the Abbott.

Wandering between the various stalls and tents after lunch and making myself more familiar with the various facilities for circus performers and assistants, I had not realised the amount of land taken up by the funfair with it's many attractions and stalls. Many of the larger attractions were already whirling around, being tested before the forthcoming grand opening.

Nearing one of the tents used by the circus workers, I noticed outside a large wicker basket containing, what I thought must be laundry and probably awaiting collection. About to walk on, I thought I could hear a small cry came from within the basket. Thinking a small cat or similar small animal might have become trapped in it, I stopped to see if I could help. Looking into the large basket and seeing nothing but various garments, I was about to be on my way, when I heard another cry. Not wanting to disturb the contents, I spied a small stick nearby. Using it to rearrange a few of the garments, a small face suddenly appeared, looking up at me.

"Please Miss, could you please get us out from here?"

Completely surprised and unable to think what to say, I could only look down at this very small face in astonishment, wondering what it could be.

"We should not be in here, can you get us out?" the small voice continued.

Still saying nothing, I could not think what to do. Finally, I managed to ask, "what or who are you?"

"I am Peter and my friend near to me is Johnathan. I think the others must be further down as I have not heard them say anything for a long time."

Still completely confused, I again managed to ask, "but what are you?"

"Marionettes, miss. Can you get us out? I think they will be coming for us soon and then we will be scolded. The water must be very hot to wash all these used garments."

"The water must be hot?" I repeated, still confused.

"The water, miss. It will scold us all to death. Please get us out quickly or it will be the end of us."

"Quicker than quickly, if you please," a deeper voice called out.

"You are marionettes?" I again asked, still confused, "but marionettes cannot talk."

"We can talk, but will not be able to talk for much longer if you hesitate any longer to help us. Will you please stop dilly-dallying and remove us all from this dreadful basket as quickly as possible?" asked the deeper voice.

Still not understanding how dummies could talk to me and wondering how I was talking to them, I used the stick to push further aside a few more of the garments. As I did so, more small figures were revealed. Seeing the painted bodies and the strings attached to the bodies, I exclaimed, "you are marionettes!"

"We know what we are, we have already told what we are, now will you please take us from this laundry basket before the men come to throw us all into the washing machine with all these dirty clothes," a nervous voice called out.

Again using the stick to push aside more of the clothing, I bent over the side of the large basket to retrieve the first two small objects. Picking each up, I looked around for somewhere to place them. An upturned nearby box seemed the nearest place I could place the small bodies. Back again at the basket and again using the stick, this time with greater care, I uncovered more garments from around three more marionettes. Freeing them and picking them up gently and carefully, I placed them with the other two.

"What shall I do now?" I asked. "Where do you live, I mean, where should you be? I can't leave you out here. It might rain."

"We are normally in that red and yellow tent, near the orange cart." said one.

"Yes," joined in another, "we were hanging from a clothes line where we normally stay between performances, when our marionette master came into the tent and was angry with us. It was because during our last performance, one of Johnathan's strings broke."

"That made me look really silly, that did," replied a dummy I thought must be the one named Johnathan. "I have never felt so embarrassed before an audience and there were small children in that audience.

It was the string connected to my leg so my left leg would not move," the marionette with the deeper voice announced. "I was supposed to do a little dance while the others stood around me and clapped, but all I could do was to shuffle around on one leg. After the show had finished, the marionette master was very angry with me, then he started finding fault with all of us. I mean, if my string breaks, how can it be my fault? I didn't make me and I certainly did not make my strings. It is the marionette master who is to blame for not looking after us as he should have."

"Goes out every night, he does," interrupted another voice. "Doesn't get back until the early hours. Always arguing and picking fights with other circus performers."

"Anyway," continued another voice, "he became angry and threw us all in a nearby basket and said he was going to get rid of us and get some different marionettes in to take our places. What a cheek? After all the service we have given him over the years. Just because we are all getting a little bit older and our joints are a little stiffer than they used to be. I mean, doesn't everyone get stiffer joints as they get older?"

"Because he was so angry and threw us all into the basket, he went off and sulked," said another voice.

"I think the real problem is," added a voice, which I thought might be a lady marionette, "I have heard that the ringmaster is not happy with the marionette master. Apparently, he considers that the act we do is too old-fashioned and marionette shows are not really popular enough with the public who come to be entertained in a circus."

"I like marionette shows," I added quickly. Then added, "if you are now all homeless, what will you all do?"

"We are unable to walk so can't do anything for ourselves," was the sad reply.

"I share a caravan with Miss Carrie-Ann who is very nice and very helpful," I said. "If I can mange to bundle you together, I could take you to the caravan we share and ask her what can be done."

"Bundle? Not too close, if you don't mind, it's just that I don't like my tummy being squeezed too much," added a concerned voice.

"I shall carry you as loosely as I can and very carefully too." I said, as I tried to put one arm around two of the dummies with another three under my other arm.

Making my way towards the caravan, I came across Mrs Hibbard who seemed to be huffing and puffing and was obviously in a great hurry.

"My dear girl, what have you got there?" she asked, bending over and trying to see the heads of the dummies.

Wondering if the dummies would speak, I quickly replied, "these had accidentally been placed in the laundry basket. I was about to take them to the caravan I share with Carrie-Ann to see what I should," but I had no time to finish.

"Take them instead to my caravan, here is the number," and she fiddled through the many pockets in her apron. Finally finding what she was looking for, she handed me a small card. "Leave them on the settee. I will look after them and see they go to a good home. Are you alright my dear, are you settling in nicely with Carrie-Ann?" Without waiting for an answer, she said, "must leave you, in a bit of a hurry, what with all the things being left to the last minute before the big opening." With that, she just swept away and was gone.

Making my way to the caravan, but getting a little lost on the way, I carefully placed each dummy on the settee. Standing back and looking at them, I said, "I noticed you did not say anything to that lady." There was a silence as each dummy lay motionless.

"I meant about how the marionette master had ill-treated you," I added, Still there was no answer. Looking closely at the dummies, each one seemed so lifeless, I wondered if they would ever speak again.

Returning to the caravan I shared, Carler-Ann was just leaving as I approached.

"How nice to see you again," she said, smiling. "And just in time, I was about to try to find you. Would you be agreeable to again visit to the gardens of Priory House sometime this afternoon? It has all been arranged and the visit is simply to collect the paperwork about the final decisions concerning the arrangements made of the merry-go -round and other smaller attractions we are providing."

Delighted to be able to help, I immediately agreed and a little later was ready and on my way. Walking briskly along Bridge Street, through the archway leading to the Priory House lawn, I was pleased to see a group of volunteers already meeting on the lawn. I was also pleased the paperwork I had come for was ready for me to collect.

Admiring the narrow stream running past the lawns with it's collection of ducks and fish, very near to the Priory House, I was surprised to see the door slightly open as I wondered past. Remembering what the doorkeeper had told me previously about keeping the door locked, I assumed he must be somewhere inside the building. Thinking I might need to talk to him about the forthcoming fair, I made my way towards the door, stopping just inside. With no sign of the tall, but stooping man who had unlocked the door for me on my previous visit, I made my way further into the hallway.

"If I make my way into the main hallway," I told myself, "he might be there." Walking through a few of the rooms and with no sign of him, I returned to the main hallway, where my attention was drawn to the main staircase leading to the upper floors. Idly wondering how many people might have walked up those very stairs over the last hundreds of years, I suddenly found myself on the first step, with my hand on the wide polished banister. Moving up each step in turn and approaching the first floor, I looked towards the ornate door I had wandered through on my previous visit. Quickly hurrying up the next flight of stairs in case it should suddenly fly open, I again waited for any sound of the doorkeeper, feeling slightly nervous about calling out in this old empty house.

Hearing nothing, I noticed to my left, a short distance and set apart from the main stairway, a much narrower set of stairs. Curious about this as it was so much smaller and so different from the main stairway, I thought it might take me to the next floor, which must be very near the attic of the building itself. I was also curious where it might lead me. Following it, I found myself on a narrow landing with three doors, very close together, with each one almost hidden behind a large wooden pillar. Looking towards the end, I could just make out in the gloom, an older door, very much smaller than the other three and with as much ornate decoration carved onto it, as the door on the first floor I had visited. Wondering why such a richly carved door would be hidden behind cobwebs and at the end of a narrow dingy corridor, I slowly walked towards it as quietly as possible, as if not wanting to disturb anybody nearby. If I open the door just a small amount, I thought, I can see what is inside and then quickly close it and return to the ground floor, satisfied the doorkeeper is not in the building. Taking a quick breath and pushing aside the worst of the cobwebs, I was very surprised and a little shocked when the door swung back as my finger lightly touched it, even though the bronze door handle had not moved.

The open door revealed a very large room with the sloping roof telling me I was obviously now in the attic of the building. At first I could not make out what I was seeing, but venturing just a short way into the room, found myself coming face to face with me. Stopping in astonishment just inside the room, I gazed at my refection in a very large and very tall mirror. Holding my breath, I waited for a short while, then looking into my reflection, I moved my right hand and waved to myself. My reflection did not move, but continued to stare at me as I was at it. Waiting for a further few seconds, I then waved my left hand hoping to see the reflection wave back at me. Again there was no movement, my reflection simply did not move. Standing there and continuing to stare at me, the reflection then suddenly seemed to come alive and waved back to me with one hand, smiling as it did so. Shocked, I was about to quickly make my way out of the room, but instead managed to remain calm, but I could feel my heart beating rapidly.

Trying again, I raised my left arm and waved. This time the reflection waved back at me, causing me to become a little more relaxed, until I realised the reflection was waving the wrong arm. Each time I waved one arm, the reflection waved back with the other arm. Lowering my arms to my side, I smiled at the mirror, which smiled back at me, but then after a few seconds, scowled at me, then after a further few seconds, stuck out it's tongue. Completely confused, I turned away and tried to avoid looking any more at that mirror and instead made my way further into the room. My path was restricted due to the room being littered with many other mirrors of all sizes and shapes, scattered throughout the large attic room, making it difficult for me to make my way further into the room.

Managing to steer my way past all the clutter, I noticed a number of mirrors were small, many others had different shaped frames, but many were very large. Some, as I walked past, showed my reflection, but others did not and I wondered if perhaps those were not mirrors at all, but simply frames containing blank glass. Continuing to my way through this maze of mirrors, I thought I had finally come to the end of the room, when I found myself in front of three large mirrors almost barring my way. The mirror to my left and the one on the right, were blank and did not show my reflection. Looking into the one in the middle and the larger of the three, my reflection did appear, then disappeared, then appeared again.

I waited to see if this reflection would be as strange as the one I had first seen when first entering the room. The reflection smiled at me, then it turned and walked into the distance, becoming smaller as it walked away. Stopping and returning after a short while and now facing me, it moved a hand, as if making a sign for me to follow. Turning back again, it walked a further short distance away, stopped, looked back at me, still waving it's hand, as if beckoning me to come closer still. In my confusion and, I think, trying to get closer, I found myself almost pushing myself against the surface of the mirror. Walking back towards me, it became both closer and larger until we were almost face to face. It extended a hand towards me, again as if wanting to assist me to follow. Without thinking, I held out my hand against the surface of the mirror and immediately felt the tightness of the grip as a hand reached through the mirror and gently guided me through. Taking a few steps forward, I found myself being led through something, I did not know what and then along a darkened passageway. A voice very close to me whispered, "you are expected, you will not be alone." Then, I felt the hand slip away from me and I realised I was alone.

Keeping very still, in case something unexpected should happen, I carefully and silently looked around, not daring to move my body or make any sound. Looking back, I thought how I must have stepped through the surface of the mirror to be here. But how was that possible, I wondered and where am I now? I am in a passageway with darkness behind me and dinginess ahead of me, apart from that, I am confused.

Walking slowly forward, I put my hand against one wall to guide myself forward in what little light there was in this small strange passageway. Coming to small wooden door, I hesitated not knowing if I should go any further. Taking a deep breath, I reached forward to turn the small handle on the door, not knowing if it would be locked. Relieved, the handle turned and I remained still, wondering if I dare to open it.

Nervously, I pushed the door just slightly, hoping to see what was on the other side before going any further. To my amazement, the small door swung itself fully open, flooding the small passageway with more light and allowing me to see more of where I was. Bending low, so I could make my way through the opening, I found myself in a very strange place. Thick wooden beams seemed everywhere about me and I thought, as I looked around and then above me, they must be a large structure supporting a roof, with the lower beams just a short distance above my head.

To one side of me was a small narrow wall, running the length of the walkway. Looking carefully over this, I was stunned to see far, far below me, a large open area. Chairs were stacked in rows and seemed to fill most of the floor area. Trying to bend my position a little and holding onto the top of the low wall, I managed to see further across the area and realised I was now high up in the attic area of Christchurch Priory and no longer in Priory House. Although I could not see the altar, I could see the side passageways with their small chapels far below me. Feeling a little dizzy at being so high, I crawled on my hands and knees to the other side of the walkway. There, for as far as I could see, was not a wall but an almost flat surface, very wide and made of bricks and plaster. In the centre was a small gangway, bordered with ropes either side. Looking at it, I thought it might be a way of walking across that part of the ceiling and looking even further, spied another smallish door in a far wall, similar to the one that had led me here into the attic of the priory.

Feeling nervous about walking along the roped gangway and across the ceiling of the priory, I slowly and carefully made my way to the far wall. Coming close to the small door, I paused, nervous about what might be on the other side. Shaking slightly, I took the handle of the door in one hand and after a short pause, turned it slowly and carefully pushed open the door just a short way. Light suddenly flowed into the space allowing me to see more of where I now was.

"Come in child," shouted a voice from somewhere beyond.

Feeling I had been discovered and would be told off, as I should not be where I was, I slowly managed to make my way through the opening, noticing there were a few steps down to a lower floor. Stepping carefully down these and looking around, I could see I was now in a large room. Looking over to the far wall I noticed a figure I did not initially see. As it rose from a chair and shuffled towards me, I burst out, "Sir, it is you."

Smiling, the figure slowly made his way towards me, supported by a long stick. The strange man I had met on the Stanpit recreation ground a short while ago and who I was now assisting in trying to recover his lost relic was now coming towards me. "You are most welcome, my child to this, my temporary dwelling."

In my astonishment, I found I could not think what to say. Then I managed to stutter, "Sir, I am not sure where I am and you have surprised me and." Pausing and swallowing, I continued, "what I am trying to say is, I seem to be lost in the attic of a strange building. I have somehow found myself very high in the attic space of Christchurch Priory and the door I have just opened was the only way I could see to find my way out."

"You are now presently in the old school room, St Michael's Loft. Have no fear of being here, you are quite safe, as am I. In olden days, boys in this classroom could on occasions watch through that window, smugglers bringing their contraband in carts across the marshes below us. From this room can you safely descend the steps to again be united with your new companions with the circus. Whilst here, I have watched you ascend the stairs of the neighbouring dwelling and approach this sacred church through a passageway atop both buildings. I have reasons to address you. First must I learn of any important news you have gained concerning the whereabouts of the sacred relic I have asked you to assist me recover. Secondly, I must remind you of my warning concerning the evil and devious wicked Cretonious, a past Abbott, but an Abbott no longer. He did once serve others. Now he serves only himself and his desire to become powerful and with that power to seek further power. In any form he may disguise himself, he must be thwarted. Not until the relic is safely in my hands, that I may then pass it onto he who must follow me, will this evil person continue to seek that which is not his to rightfully own."

"Sir, a man did approach me whilst I was out on the marshes. He asked about you and said it would comfort him to learn you are safe. He also asked if I could give him any details so he could find and visit you and claimed he was only interested in your safety."

"He has made a mistake in making himself known to you. Now will you become aware if such an enquiry about myself shall again befall you in whatever disguise he shall use and with whatever words he might speak. There will come a time shortly, when I must present the sacred relic to my successor that it might be protected from prying eyes, as my priory has protected it for many hundreds of years. This is the reason for my travelling to this place and this must I accomplish before an important forthcoming religious festival."

"Before a forthcoming religious festival?" I repeated, wondering when this would be.

"Before the summer shall end," the Abbott said, as if understanding what I was thinking.

"Go now, that door and those steps will take you down to the where you will be safe and allow your return to your new circus friends."

Looking at him, I wondered if I should ask about the people in the circus who seemed to know about my joining them, but the old man had already turned and was slowly making his way back to his chair, leaning on his stick. Pausing to look through the window and across the marshes, he added, more to himself than to me, "time does flow too quickly, the relic must be found soon, it must be found soon."

Seeing him turn towards his chair, I made my way to the stairway, which I hoped would lead me down to a more familiar part of the priory. Walking carefully down the many narrow stone steps in this circular tower, I thought of the many generations of school children who had to make this journey a number of times, each and every school day.

With the sun shining and the birds flying in and out of the nearby branches, I almost ran the short distance to the recreation ground and finally, my caravan.

Secret doors in the walls of the old Norman church.

Chapter Five

The George Inn, finding the relic,
circus acts, the professor's dummies.

Excited by the first day of the opening performance of the circus, although I knew some of the larger attractions in the neighbouring funfair had been whirling around for the past two days, I made my way towards all the excitement. As packers, unpackers and chair arrangers went about their work to make sure every item was where it should be, I found Mrs Hibbard and asked if I could help with some of the smaller jobs. "Make sure the sawdust is carefully raked on the inside of the ringside barriers," she said. "A smooth service always looks nice and the ponies prefer it." Armed with a rake, I got to work. Finishing that job after an hour, I asked if there was anything else I could do.

"Sit by the ringside and look around to see if you think there is anything we might have forgotten," she advised. "Sometimes someone unfamiliar with a circus can see things we might have missed."

Happy to do so, I relaxed in a chair next to the front row and wondered if I might be able to stay there and enjoy the whole show. Then I reminded myself, although I was happy to have this job for the summer holidays and a very interesting one, I had also promised the elderly Abbott Joshua, I would do all I could to help find the lost relic. Hopefully I can return it to him that he might hand to another person, known only to him in a secret place. When that would be, I did not know. I did not even know what the item I was searching for looked like. The two Richards I had met, I remembered, had told me the monkey had carried it from the trapeze artists' ropes and had suggested I ask the monkey trainer. Just then I spied Mrs Hibbard fussing and flapping as she tried to make sure every little thing was in its place before the opening. Calling out as she noticed me approaching her, she said, "my dear, as I look around at the many props our performers are insisting on using, they seem to get bigger and bigger each season and there so many more of them than the season last year."

"Mrs Hibbard," I said, trying not to interrupt her, "I was wondering if you could tell me about where I might find the performer with the monkey act. I should like to speak to him if I can."

"Oh no, dear. We don't have a monkey act. The monkey you probably mean is a personal pet, although that performer, Pedro, does sometimes let his monkey delight the younger children with a few tricks. Pedro is a performer of conjuring tricks."

Directing me to the part of the circus grounds where I might find him, I made my way there, still unfamlier with many of the areas used by the circus performers. Seeing a man fitting Mrs Hibbard's description, I approached him and was just about to ask about the monkey.

"Not now, young, lady," he said, seeing me approach. "I am practising a new routine with my clubs, as well you can see."

"With your clubs?" I asked, wondering he meant.

Bending down to retrieve a large wooden object, that to me looked like a skittle, then two more, I said, "I am sorry to disturb you," but then stopped as the man started to throw one into the air, followed by a second and then a third. Catching each one in turn with the flick of one hand, he suddenly stopped, turned to me and asked, "what is it you want? I intend to practice and I do not have much time."

"Only about the monkey," I quickly said. "Two of the circus performers, the Richard Twins, told me they had seen your monkey with an object lost by an elderly man. He has asked me to help him find it. I believe it is very important to him."

Preparing to again toss the first of three clubs into the air, he paused, turned towards me and said, "if it is indeed the same thing you are looking for, try the George Inn in Castle Street, they have it. Don't know if they want to keep it. Strange thing, light as a feather when my monkey brought it to me, when I later went to pick it up, weighed a ton. When a friend came in to help me lift it, it was again as light as a feather. George Inn up the road, corner of the high street is where you will find it. Ask for the landlady, Mrs Tropase and mention my name. I am Pedro, finest conjurer in the south. Now be off with you and let me get on with what I need to do before the start of the performance this afternoon."

As I had some time before lunch and my meeting with Carrie-Ann and knowing the High street was just a short distance away, I thanked him and hurriedly made my way towards the High Street.

The door to the George Inn was shut and the inn appeared to be empty, but a narrow alleyway running beside the inn caused me to wonder if there might be another entrance to the rear of the building. Coming to the end of the alleyway, an unfastened rear gate led me to a garden.

"Can I help you?" asked a voice somewhere near to me as I slowly made my way through the garden.

"I am hoping to meet a Mrs Tropase," I said.

"You have found her, I am Mrs Tropase," called out a large lady, arranging flowers on one of a number of tables.

"It is about an object bought here by a circus performer, I only know him as Pedro, but he told me you would know him. His monkey found something that might be what an elderly gentleman recently lost and is very important to him. He has asked me to help find it and hopefully return it to him."

"If it is the same thing I believe it is, we put it on a stone shelf, as it was so heavy. Couldn't lift it myself, needed the help of a few customers."

Turning and making her way back into the inn, she called back to me, "this way, dear."

Following her, she continued, "Pedro, sometimes brings me objects from his travels around the country, as we already have our own collection of unusual objects on show. He did not know what that item is, neither do we."

Following her through a door leading into the Inn, she stopped and pointed, "there it is. I don't know what you can do with it as it is so heavy and I have heard it now and then make strange noises. If it is the same thing your old gentleman has lost, you are most welcome to it."

Never having seen it before, I approached it slowly. I thought it to be made of metal and with two small connected round dials on the front, a hollow space in the middle and another dial on one side. On the top and closer to the rear of the object were a few strange signs and letters, which I had not seen before. Bending my neck slightly, there was a small face protruding from the rear of the object. Touching it gently, I found as my fingers came closer, the object slid slightly away across the stone shelf. Taking my hand away, the object slowly began to change to a dull purple colour.

"Well, that is interesting, that never happened before, it was a greyish colour when it was brought here," the lady exclaimed. "You come back later this afternoon, we will have our handyman here. He can give a hand with lifting it off the shelf, although how you are going to manage to carry it away, I do not know."

Thanking her and looking at it again, I wondered how I would be able to take it back to the circus. I did also wonder how Pedro, the conjurer had managed to carry it to the Inn, then there was the monkey and the three men who had first carried it from the field across the marshes. It was all very confusing.

Lunch first and I was interested to see many of the performers were already wearing the costumes they would be using for their forthcoming performances.

The opening performance of the circus was a great success, according to the laughter I heard, the three comedians and the Richards twins, I thought, amusing. Mentioning to Carrie-Ann my impressions of the opening performance, I asked if there was any way for me to help. I did hope I might become more involved in guiding the Shetland ponies around the ring and assist in selecting which children from the audience would be chosen to ride one or two of them.

Later, making way back to the George Inn, which I was pleased to see was now open with seating arrangements outside in the sun. The handyman was waiting for me, but informed me, "I tried to see how heavy this object was likely to be and found it practically has no weight at all. Light as a feather. You don't need my help at all."

Pleased that I would be able to take the object away by myself and thanking him for his trouble, I carefully put my hand around the item wondering how best to hold it due to it's strange shape and remembering that when I had tried to touch it earlier, it had somehow moved away from me.

I need not have worried, as the item was light and seemed to almost lift itself off the shelf. Wrapping it in a scarf I had brought with me, I made my way towards the front door, which had previously been open. Now it was closed and however much I tried to turn and then pull the handle, it refused to budge. Turning, I looked around for Mrs Tropase, but both she and the handyman were nowhere in sight and I did not want to call out to her. Thinking they might both be in the rear of the building, I made my way there, but noticed the large back gate was now closed and locked. The door of the far building of the inn was open so perhaps they were in that building. Walking in between the tables and chairs and towards a few large barrels to the rear of the room, only to realise too late a large trap door, just in front of me, was open. Without being able to save myself, I felt myself falling into the dark space below. What saved me from injury was a large thick item, perhaps a mattress, on the floor.

Lying were I had fallen for a moment, I looked around, trying to see where I was. There were a number of other barrels close to me and there appeared to be the entrance to a tunnel or opening, further along the wall, but in the gloom, I could not be sure. Managing to get myself up and relieved I was still holding the relic, I looked for a way of somehow climb back up into the room. There appeared none except to climb on the barrels, but they were too heavy to move. Calling out, I hoped Mrs Tropase would now be somewhere near and hear me. Shouting again, I heard nothing. Perhaps the dingy entrance I had seen at the far end of the room, might be the only way for me to find a way out.

Stepping carefully over the mattress and across the stone floor, I noticed a dull light coming from somewhere above me, which allowed me to see a little way ahead. Stopping and looking through the open entrance, I seemed to be looking into a tunnel. I had no difficulty in walking slowly through the first part as it was both wide and high. Where it would lead me to and where it would end, I could not know.

Walking on, thankful even for a dull light, I thought I could sometimes faint hear noises from traffic somewhere above my head. Walking slowly further on, I came to a set of stone steps leading up and at the top, a wooden door. The steps, although very old and worn, seemed safe, so carefully walking up and pushing against the door, I was disappointed to find it to be fastened from the other side. A small dusty window to one side let in more daylight and also allowed me to see out a little way. The old ruins of the stone castle keep, high on a hill meant I must be below the old court house. Returning again down the stone steps, I wandered further on along the passageway, which was becoming gloomier the further I went.

Suddenly light from an opening somewhere allowed me to see more of the tunnel ahead. It was as if someone had opened a door. When I looked down, I noticed the shadows on the wall were moving as I moved. Looking down at the object I was carrying, the scarf had fallen away and the bright light was coming from the object itself. As it was so bright and causing me difficulty in seeing, I tried to again wrap the scarf around the relic, but it made little difference. The light continued to shine almost as bright as before. Relieved about now being able to see where I was going, but confused as to how such a strong light could come from an old relic. I wandered on, hoping to find an end to this tunnel as quickly as possible.

Walking a further short distance, I found myself near to another set of steps leading upto an old wooden door. A large rusty bolt first barred my way, but I managed to slide it back, slowly pushing open the door with difficulty, but just far enough to see what was beyond. I thought I might be looking into a basement of a ruined building as everywhere looked so old and damaged. Making my way carefully through the rubble and discarded objects, I made my way across the room until I spied very old wooden steps in the corner.

Walking carefully up these and treading on the edge of each wooden step as they did not look too safe and pushing open an old door, I found myself entering a smaller room with various pieces of old furniture stacked against one wall. There seemed to be no other door for me to continue, but then looking up a short distance above my head, I noticed a trap door, one of a pair. A barrel just under it was small enough for me to climb onto it and then pushing up with both hands, I managed to open one door up far enough for me to heave myself up onto a very dirty floor. Very close to me, were a number of sacks of stones and rubble with two positioned on the other trap door, perhaps to hide it.

Making my way carefully between the various sacks and other large dusty items, I came to an old window opening in the stone wall. Looking out, I could see I was close to the side door of the priory and the edge of the graveyard. Turning back to the room, I noticed that as well as the nearby sacks of rubble, there were also a number of wooden beams of various lengths and sizes. Perhaps I was in a building used to store building materials for repairs to the priory church.

Some of the nearby rooms were without roofs, so clambering through these, I managed to find a door and could finally make my way out into the priory graveyard, with the relic safely tucked under my arm.

Glancing up to the very top of the tower above me, I thought I could see a large bird, similar to the buzzard I had seen on the marshes. Perched at the very top, it seemed to be looking directly down at me, which did scare me a little. Walking through the graveyard, I nervously looked back, but the bird was no longer to be seen.

Continuing along the narrow path bordering the stream running past the graveyard, I made my way back to the circus and the caravan. Clutching the relic across my chest and covered under both arms, I wondered when I would be able to again meet the Abbot and return to him this sacred relic.

Finally finding myself back at the caravan, I looked for an appropriate place to hide the relic. Seeing none, I spied a large trunk of old clothes which I thought might be a temporary hiding place until I could find something more secure. Removing a few items of clothing from the top, I pushed the relic further down, hoping no-one would bother to disturb the contents. Thinking I must quickly return after lunch, I would try to find a more appropriate place. I hoped the object would not make any noise, flash any lights or do anything to attraction the attention of any passerby. Leaving the caravan, I set off looking for Carrie-Ann, as I had been told she wished to talk to me over lunch about the afternoon performance.

Sitting next to Carrie-Ann for lunch, she began to tell me how she had been with the circus for many years of her life, training as a trapeze artist from a very early age with her family and how that had ended when, in later life, she had a fall. The rope she was about to catch broke, causing her to fall into the safety net, but then bounced out of that and onto the floor below, causing her injuries and ending her career. The rope maker was fired as he had not inspected and renewed the rope as he should. Now, she continued, she helps her father, a part owner of the circus, with the day-to-day running of events. She also hinted the afternoon performance might involved me, which did cause me to wonder what she could mean. As soon as lunch was finished, she asked I go directly to the main marquee and the ringmaster would explain what he wanted me to do. In my excitement at the thought of being part of the circus acts, I forgot about the clothes basket.

Along with everyone else, I was excited at the start of the afternoon performance. I had already been given a seat number, where I would sit, in the front row and at the end of that row. As families started taking their seats and the entrances crowed with excited parents and children, being in the huge marquee and looking for their seat numbers, the empty seats were gradually all filled up. With an expected hush, the ringmaster entered in the arena in full dress uniform of scarlet coat and black top hat with an accompanying sound from the musicians. In his hand he carried a long black whip, which I think is to show his status and to 'crack' when announcing the various acts and performers.

As the band started to play, the circus performers paraded in turn through the arena, entering from the main entrance on my right and leaving by an opposite exit. The crowd settled back to enjoy the afternoon. The first acts were the clowns and I was amused by the first three clowns, each wearing baggy pants, colourful jackets and faces painted a multitude of colours. Each one wore an identical black 'bowler' or 'derby' hat, but in different sizes. The rather plump clown wore a very wide hat, the thin clown wore a very narrow black bowler hat and the middle clown wore a hat somewhere in between. Starting with their usual introduction, one announced, "there's me Albert, that be my name, I'm the tall, rather plump one, then there be Bertrum, he be the thin short one, then there be Danial, he be the one in the middle, not too tall nor too small, not too plump nor too thin."

The act then proceeded with all clowns bending so far forward, their hats fell to the ground. As each clown bent down to pick up the nearest hat and putting it on, each realised he is now wearing the wrong hat. The plump clown had upon his head a very narrow hat, the thin clown had upon his head a very wide hat that covered his eyes, so he couldn't see anything and the clown in the middle seemed satisfied. Each took off his hat, gave it to his neighbour and demanded back their hat. Again the hats did not fit. Continually getting and putting on another wrong hat, caused the audience to laugh due to the constant changing of hats and the expressions and frustration of the clowns.

Expecting more, the audience waited for what was to follow. A tray of cakes was produced with the tallest of the clowns announcing that as he was the tallest, he had more right than the others to eat more cakes. Bending down and picking up one leg, the smaller clown, asked loudly, "why has it always got to be me what is the smallest one of the three.

What about someone else taking their turn, so I can sometimes be the tall one?"

With the three having an argument why the smallest clown always had to be the smallest and therefore only allowed to eat less cakes from the table than the two other clowns, the audience laughed at their ongoing arguments and sound effects. With their props causing loud bangs whenever one clown fell over, whistle noises as another tried to speak, causing him to give up trying, the smaller one eventually walked off, making the audience believe that 'he was being put upon'. Having walked away from the arena, he emerged a short while later, taller than anyone else walking on wooden legs hidden under his trousers. "Now I am the taller of the three and can have the most cakes on the table. One of you is now the smallest, so you will get the least number of cakes to eat from the table."

When the three had finally finished their act, judged by the laughter to have been a success, the ringmaster entered the ring to announce that a number of animals would be led around the ring and by a member of the audience, decided by where the searchlight would eventually stop. As the searchlight bounced around the rows of people, it soon came to stop on me. Now realising what Carrie-Ann had meant, I nervously left my seat, stepped over the low wall and into the arena. Waiting as the ringmaster came over to me and handed me the reins of the first animal. I noticed it was the same Shetland pony I had previously taken to the marshes.

Slightly nervous of so many people looking at me, I gently led the pony around the ring with the ringmaster guiding the others to follow. Having led the animals while the small band played loudly, the ringmaster asked the audience for an applause for this 'special' member of the audience. As the music ended, I led the animals out of the ring.

Somewhat relieved to be out of the spotlight, but missing the rest of the various acts which were to follow, I led the Shetland pony back towards the animal shelter with the other animals in tow. Once there and handing them over to the various handlers, I began to make my way back to the marquee, but was interrupted by a voice calling to me.

"You be her?" called out a voice from behind me. "I thought you might be, soon as I saw you standing there, I thought to myself, you must be her."

Turning, I noticed two strange looking men coming towards me. Both were dressed in similar costumes, the pattern on their shirts rather like a chessboard and each wearing blue baggy trousers with coloured patches. Although dressed identical, the tall thin one looked very different from his very short and very round companion.

"Excuse us miss, you be the new girl to help us with our act? It will only be for a few days until our assistant is better."

"I don't think so." I replied, "that is, no-one has said anything to me about anything like that."

"Not the ringmaster, he didn't tell you about our act needing someone for the next few performances?" the taller one asked.

"Let us first introduce ourselves," interrupted the smaller of the two. "I be named Mr Timpani, that be my name from the day I was born, that be."

"And I be named Mr Tompani. Always has been and always will be and none can disagree with that. Is that not so, Mr Timpani?" asked the shortest of the two, looking up at his companion.

Both then turned their attention to me and looked expectantly at me, grinning as if waiting for an answer.

"I am Jemima Jones," I answered, looking at the two looking at me, still grinning.

"You don't mind?" asked the taller one.

"No need to mind, no need to mind at all," interrupted the smaller person looking up at me. "I only had to take one look at you to see that you are the sort of person, who after the first two of three throws would, how can I explain it, get use to it, I believe that is the appropriate phrase to use. Would you not agree with that, Mr Timpani, two or three throws, wouldn't you say?"

"Undoubtedly," replied his friend, "although four or five throws might be the right number for some assistants, makes them feel a little more comfortable."

"Right then, we agree of four or five throws and you will feel as right as rain. Would you not agree, Mr Timpani, right as rain?"

"Now that is decided, we start our act in under the hour, so perhaps we should think about a suitable costume for you. While I think about that, the most important thing I can say to you when we make a throw, you should not move."

"Oh I think, Mr Tompani, the young lady would know that. It is after all, common sense. A person is unlikely to even think about any movement of any kind when a sharp knife comes whizzing towards them."

Just then the familiar round figure of Mrs Hibbard strode firmly past us.

"My dear," she said kindly, "you were such a success carrying out that small routine, we would like you perform it in each performance while you are with us."

"Perform at each performance?" repeated the taller of the two. "Oh no, I am very sorry, you can't have her. Mr Tompani and I have just discussed having this young lady in our knife throwing act and believe she will be most suitable for the act. Did we not agree on that very fact, Mr Tompani, that this young lady would be most suitable to stand close to our target board as we aim our knives around her."

Shocked at what I was hearing, Mrs Hibbard quickly interrupted him.

"I am very sorry, Mr Tompani and Mr Timponi, but you will have to look elsewhere for a new assistant. This young lady is certainly not going to be part of any knife throwing act." Then turning to me and holding my hand, she announced, "you come with me, my dear and well away from any knife throwing that goes on in this circus." With that, she almost pulled me away from the disappointed two.

With a number of circus performers and assistants continually approaching Mrs hibbard with their suggestions or complaints, she soon left me to deal with the ones she felt to be the most pressing.

Left to myself, I wandered slowly back to the caravan, and was pleased to find Carrie-Ann now back and immersed in writing in a notebook. Seeing me, she congratulated me on my role in the ring and making suggestions of where else I could help over the next few weeks. Looking around I was horrified to see the basket I had hidden the relic now missing. Trying to remain calm, I asked, "I see the basket containing the clothes has gone."

Without out looking up from what she was writing, Carrie-Ann said, "the basket? oh that has been taken away to the props tent."

"The props tent?" I repeated, trying not to sound too concerned.

"Yes, strangely enough, the man who came to collect it, for some reason could not lift it. He said it was so heavy, he would have to get two other men to help him take it away."

Saying nothing, I wondered how I could ask where it might have been taken, without being asked why I had this sudden interest in the basket. "It was only because I had left a small notebook on it," I said.

"A small notebook?" was the reply. "I did not notice it. The basket is probably now in the main props tent awaiting collection tomorrow with all the other luggage, due to be taken to our next destination. Your notebook is probably still with the basket"

A knock on the caravan door revealed Mrs Hibbard as she poked her head in, saying, "evening ladies. Miss Jemima, I am sorry for having to leave you to attend to other matters. I wonder if you could help us after supper. There are a few costumes we need for the performance tomorrow, but they have mistakenly been put into a basket with other costumes and have been taken to the props tent for dispatch tomorrow. There are twelve of them and are all coloured green. You won't have any trouble finding them. Just separate them from the others and I will arrange collection before the baskets are due to be collected tomorrow."

"There you are," said Carrie-Ann, "while you are there, you will get the opportunity to retrieve your notebook."

"After supper?" I said, getting up and joining Mrs Hibbard, thankful for this opportunity to try to find the relic.

"That's right, my dear, it won't take you long to locate the distinctive green basket and retrieve the costumes." With that she turned and closed the caravan door.

Later, with supper eaten and darkness approaching, I made my way towards the props tent, following the directions given by Carrie-Ann.

Having first to search for the light switch, I found the props tent to be much larger than I thought it would be and had not realsied it was joined by small corridors to other similar tents, each full of circus props and old scenery. As well as a number of baskets all stored close to each other in the first tent, presumably awaiting collection tomorrow, there was also a collection of larger props and stacks of chairs. My first concern was to find the clothes basket taken from the caravan. Looking at the jumble of other baskets, some standing on other larger boxes and baskets, I looked in vain for the basket removed from our caravan.

Behind two large wooden cut-outs of old castle walls in an adjoining tent, I noticed a very large trunk, covered in thick dust, with places for locks and secured with a very wide strap. Next to it was another similar trunk, secured with two straps and a broken lock. Both trunks, I noticed had similar labels attached, showing the various countries the trunks had visited, I suppose by ships to all corners to the world. One faded label bore the words, 'Professor Malani, optical illusions'.

The single light in the top of the tent did not allow me to see too much on this side of the castle walls as most of the area was quite dark. Walking on, I accidentally walked into an umbrella stand, knocking it over and causing a resounding noise that echoed around the large tent. Picking it up, I was about to walk on when I thought I could hear a knocking sound coming from somewhere nearby.

Turning to see the cause, the sound stopped. I was on my way to an adjoining tent when the sound started again. It was a simple knock, then there was silence for a short while. A second similar knocking sound appeared to come from somewhere nearby. Puzzled and a little nervous, I again stopped to listen. There was a silence, then the knocking sound could be heard throughout the tent.

Despite being a little nervous and alone in a large tent, I made an effort to try to find out where the sound was loudest. Retracing my steps back to the other side of the wooden castle wall cut-outs, I thought the knocking to be coming from the large trunks with the travel labels. Becoming closer, the sounds grew louder. Standing there, listening and pondering what I should do, I looked again at the old straps. Thinking I could undo just one, open the lid just a little to see the cause of the noise and then tell someone. Trying to unfasten the buckle, the old strap broke and slid to the floor.

Standing back a pace, I waited then taking a deep breath, held out one hand to carefully lift the lid just a short distance. Lifting it up a little, pausing then lifting it a little further, the lid suddenly flew up as if released on a spring, almost like a 'jack-in-the-box'. Flying up and banging against the wooden wall, the lid caused a loud noise. Clouds of dust flew up into the air and over me, causing me to quickly close my eyes. Waiting for the dust to clear and opening my eyes, I was startled to see a strange figure had emerged from the trunk and was now almost standing in front of me with the lower half still hidden in the trunk. I was so shocked, I could not think what to do. Stepping back, I could only gaze at this strange figure I thought must be a lifelike dummy, dressed in clothes I had never seen before. With the eyes starring at me, the mouth began to move.

"Professor," it shouted out loudly. "I am yours to command. What do you wish of me, my master?"

Bewildered that the thing could talk, I wondered if the dummy contained a recording or a talking machine. Saying nothing, I waited, still unsure what I should do. My feeling was to quickly leave the tent and tell someone.

As I remained silent, the machine, or whatever it was, started to sway from side to side. "Professor, I am here with my companion, we await your instructions." Slowly, the dummy stopped swaying and slowly turned it's head to look from side to side in a jerky manner.

"Professor, my companion awaits, where is my companion?" Then turning, again in a jerky manner as if the head was about to fall off, it looked towards my direction and asked, "where is the professor?"

Still saying nothing and wondering what I should do or say, I finally managed to blurt out, "what are you?"

"What am I? what am I? what am I? I am Samidi, assistant to the professor. Where is my companion Talushi?" We stay together, we assist the professor together. Where is Talushi?" the dummy repeated.

"I don't know of any Talushi, what is it?" I asked, standing back a few paces and wondering how I was able to be talking to such a strange figure. Just then, a knocking noise sounded from the other trunk.

"Talushi is knocking. He wishes to be free of his concealment," the strange figure added, as the hands and arms began to slowly move upwards, again in a very jerky manner. "You have not released him as you have me and I see not the professor. He will announce us. Professor, professor," it began to shout and I thought, becoming a little erratic.

Completely confused, I felt the only thing to do was to quickly leave the tent and try to find someone. Turning I began to walk away when the voice continued, "do not leave us, do not leave us. The professor did not leave us."

Stopping and turning I found the courage to call out, "but what are you, who are you?"

"Spirits from a time past to serve the professor," was the answer, as if that explained everything. "My companion must now breathe the air I breathe. He must now accompany me. I cannot be alone."

"My companion must now breathe the air?" I began to say, still not thinking very clearly and wondering what that might mean. Trying to remain calm, I approached the other trunk and started to fiddle with the two buckles fastening the two straps. Being very old and weak and with my hands shaking, they broke and fell to the floor. Standing back slightly, I lifted the lid and waited for the lid to fly up with dust everywhere as did the lid on the other trunk. Instead the lid slowly lifted itself up with a face appearing at the opening and looking up at me. As the lid fully opened, the face became a figure, similar to the other one, quickly growing higher and higher until it was as high as the other figure.

"I am Talushi, I obey the commands of the professor. I await his first command."

As I watched, again slightly nervous as to what would happen next, the dummy started to turn it's head in a jerky motion to the left and then to the right as if looking for something. Then everything stopped and the head fell slightly forward, reminding me of a rundown clockwork figure. Both figures were now silent and still, with their heads dropping slightly forward as if ready to fall. Concerned as to what might happen, I remained silent, then when both dummies continued to remain still, I said very loudly, "hello." There being no answer and no sound, I again said "hello," but louder.

Still the dummies stayed silent.

Looking at both their faces, I shouted, "the professor."

At the mention of the word 'professor', both dummies seemed to come alive, with each making jerky movements with their heads and arms.

"The professor is not here," I shouted, then thought that was the wrong thing to say as they might again become lifeless. Instead, one repeated, slowly, "professor not here?"

"When did you last obey the professor's commands?" I asked, not really expecting an answer I could understand or that the dummy would understand what I was asking.

The dummy who had said he was a spirit and seemed to find it easier to speak, replied, "obey professor commands, many, many leagues ago, from the old country."

Wondering what was meant be the word 'league', I continued, "many, many leagues ago may mean the professor is sadly no longer with us," not wanting to say that judging by the very old labels on the two trunks, he may have passed away some months or even years ago.

"Passed away some months or years ago?" the spirit or dummy suddenly announced.

Shocked that the spirit seemed to know what I was thinking, I tried to think, but could not be sure if I had said the sentence softly to myself or had only thought it. As I wondered what I could, or should say, the head of the dummy moved slightly in my direction. "Spirits from old country. Professor gave Holy Man gifts for spirits, Holy Man gave spirits to Professor. Spirits return to Holy Man in old country if professor never return."

At that moment, I thought I heard a sound of someone approaching the tent. Seeing the two figures standing in the trunks, I quickly made my way to the entrance of the tent. Just in time, as Mrs Hibbard was making her way towards me. Seeing me, she announced, "just on my way to my caravan, but thought I should just pop in to see how you are getting on and if you have managed to find those costumes."

Thanking her and hoping she would not chose to enter the tent, I replied, "not found them yet, but I will and place them as you asked." Then I thought to take the opportunity to ask her about the trunks. "I was wondering about the name Professor Malani, I noticed the name on the labels of two very old trunks."

"Professor Malani? That was a very long time ago, probably even before my time with the circus. I know the name as he was famous even then, he did an act named 'optical illusions'. I remember he was well-known for having two assistants from India and together, they would do various illusions. That was many years ago. You say we still have two of his trunks here, after all these years?"

"Yes," I said, hoping she would not stop to look at them. Unfortunately, she did. "Just show me where they are and I can have them removed." Following me, I was greatly relieved as we approached the two trunks, to see both were now closed and the figures gone. Stepping closer, Mrs Hibbard, bent down to the lift the lid of one and I was surprised and confused to see the trunk to be completely empty. Lifting the lid of the second trunk, also empty, she added, "I had no idea these old trunks were still with us. Tomorrow I will have someone collect them, they are too old to be of any value today and they are taking up too much room here." Turning to leave, she announced, "well my dear, it is getting too late to look for those costumes at this hour, I'll see you back to your caravan now and after breakfast tomorrow morning, you can continue to look for them." With that she escorted me out, switching off the light. I had no choice but to follow her back to my caravan and then to bed.

Chapter Six

A visit to Highcliffe castle
and Professor Tabalti's toy collection.

Upon waking up, I was looking forward to breakfast with Carrie-Ann, but couldn't wait to finish so I could continue searching for the missing basket. Hoping no-one had moved or disturbed it and the relic was still where I had hidden it and being asked by Mrs Hibbard to find the missing green costumes, gave me the excuse to search for the basket. I wondered if I had done the sensible thing in hiding the relic there.

Finishing breakfast and making my way back to the props tent, I was disappointed to discover the baskets had been moved and despite my searching, were nowhere in the tent. Returning to the caravan, I was relieved to see Carrie-Ann writing in her notebook at her desk. Telling her of the missing basket containing the costumes and the basket containing my notebook, she listened and then explained, "the circus will be holding a few events during the next few weeks in the grounds of the nearby Highcliffe Castle. A few of the larger events will also be held on the grounds overlooking Mudeford beaches. Some circus equipment has already been taken to the castle and the missing baskets you mention might have been taken with them by mistake. After you have given the animals their morning exercise, I can arrange for you to be taken to the castle together with our next trip. Perhaps you can find the missing items and be back in time for lunch."

Relieved I would get another opportunity to continue the search, I made my way to the animal stables, looking forward to taking the animals for their early morning daily exercise across the marshes.

With that done and the weather staying sunny, my trip to the nearby Highcliffe Castle was uneventful and as I approached the building, I was most impressed with the building and the views of the Isle of Wight. Already I could see many arrangements being made for the forthcoming events in the castle grounds as tents were being erected and seating set out before the various displays. Beginning my search for the baskets, I noticed many scattered around the grounds, so set about searching for the missing ones.

Highcliffe Castle.

Despite my searching, I became concerned the ones I was looking for appeared to be missing. Asking if there where any other baskets stored elsewhere, I was informed certain baskets and other items not needed were now being stored in a room in the castle. Welcoming the opportunity to explore inside the Castle, I quickly made my way through the large impressive front entrance and into the first of the various rooms.

The baskets and other items, some awaiting return to the circus were stored in the main large room. My disappointment continued as despite searching all the baskets in the room, the two I was so desperately seeking were not there. Sinking into a nearby chair, I wondered where else I could search. The baskets were not in the circus props tent, they were not in the castle or the grounds. Where, I wondered, was the basket containing the relic and was it still safe?

Sitting back, I waited as I had no means to return to the circus until others were ready to return with a few of the unwanted baskets and other items. Looking around the large room, I thought about the many exciting celebrations and dances that would have been held in this very room, probably as a ballroom in the past, with the ladies and gentlemen dressed in their finery. In the far corner, I spied a narrow door I had not yet noticed, quite plain and shorter than the others, which were all so large and decorated. Curious, I wondered if it led to anywhere interesting. There was no means of entry that I could see, not even a door handle. Interested to see what might lie behind the door, I found myself walking towards it.

The door, which I had thought to be coloured white, I now saw to be coloured green with a strange surface. Touching the door and running my fingers down the bright surface, nothing happened, then silently and slowly, the door swung towards me, almost knocking against me. Quickly standing back, I waited for the door to stop moving. Beyond the door I could just make out the beginning of a circular staircase in a round stone tower. The area was quite dark, but stepping forward and looking up, I could see the stairway went around and around in circles, up and up, so far that I could not the see the top. Forgetting for a moment about the baskets, I found myself stepping up onto the first step and holding the stair rail and looked up. Suddenly I found myself being whisked up the stairway as it appeared to twist itself around. Around and around it turned like a corkscrew, but my legs were not moving. Rising higher and higher, I now clutched the rail tightly with both hands, confused as to what was taking me up the stairway. Looking up, I could see I was quickly coming to the very top, when there was a slight bang. The stairway seemed to tremble and the whole thing came to a sudden stop. Still holding on tightly with both hands, I waited in case something else might happen.

After a few moments, I nervously stepped off the step I was on and onto a narrow landing. In front of me was a small door, similar to the one below and again with no handle. I waited, then reached out and carefully touching the strange surface as I had done before. The door silently opened fully inwards, leaving me peering into a darkened room.

Waiting a few moments, a little nervous still, I called out, "is anyone there?" As the room was in darkness, I did not expect an answer, but waited a few moments as I was not sure what else I should do. Then, I heard a 'rustling' sound from somewhere in the darkened room.

"Only us shadows," a gravel sounding voice called out. "There is no room here, we are full up so you might as well go away again."

"Only us shadows?" I heard myself say.

"Sh, you mustn't talk or she will know we are here, although it is probably too late for that now," a voice, not too far from me whispered. Then the voice became louder, "young lady, we know who you are because we have seen you walking around the castle grounds."

"She is the young lady with that man following her, the one I told you about," another voice called out.

"You the young lady with a man who follows you?" a different but stern voice called out.

"Who follows me?" I repeated, still not seeing who was speaking.

"Yes and we do not like him either, do we Cedric?"

"Cedric?" I repeated, still searching the darkness for the speakers.

"I am Cedric, but I am not going to talk to you until I know more about you," a different voice called out.

"Why won't you speak to me and I still cannot see you," I almost shouted out, desperate to see who were these people calling to me.

"You can't see me because as with my friends here, I am a black shadow and this is a black room, that is to say, a room in complete darkness."

"What is a black shadow?" I asked, trying to peer further into the gloom of the room.

"A black shadow is a shadow that is black and not any other colour. Anyway, I think all here in this room will agree with me and think that to be a very silly question. Did you think a black shadow would be coloured red, or any other colour, for that matter?"

"I am so confused. I am talking to a few persons I cannot see and they are saying strange things." I was becoming more nervous.

"If you strike a match from the box of matches and light up that old oil lamp on the table somewhere before you, you might be able to see us. We are on the walls, but we are not persons, so let us get that straight from the start. Persons are people and people are those selfish beings who have gone off and left us here."

"Left you here?" I was becoming more confused and still a little scared, so tried to make my way towards the table and feel about the top for the matches. Finding a box and managing to strike one match, I put it against the wick of the lamp. At once a warm glow lit up the part of the room nearest me, allowing me to see I was in a very large attic room.

"Of course they left us, why else would we be here? If we were still attached to them, we would not be here, would we? That is what I said and that is what I meant, left us, let there be no doubt about that."

"I still do not understand," I muttered, wondering if I should make my way back down the circular stairway, but then turning, noticed the door had silently shut itself behind me.

"I shall explain. Please listen to what I am about to tell you. We are shadows who have been left, that is detached, from those to whom we were once attached. Is that the correct way of putting it, Archibald? To whom we were attached?" the speaker asked.

"Thinking about it, I suppose that would be the best way to describe the situation," a deep voice called out from the far corner of the dark room.

"That was Archibald," the voice continued. "He has been here the longest."

"But how can you be detached from someone?" I asked.

"That is something we continually discuss and we each have our own theory, it somehow just happened. It is not as if we said something to upset our other parts."

"Said something to the other parts? Shadows cannot talk."

"You mean we are not talking to you now. If that is the case then you are not hearing us. No, not to humans, we don't speak. That would make no sense at all. Sometimes when we are being dragged cross the ground because our owners are walking aimlessly about on a hot sunny day, we sometimes find ourselves being knocked onto other shadows also being dragged across the ground, Then we say sorry, or excuse me. Would you say that is the best way to describe the situation, Archibald?"

"I do believe the way you have described the situation to be the best way to describe the situation you are presently attempting to describe the situation to the young lady," the voice replied.

"This is all very silly and complete nonsense," I called out in frustration. "I cannot see you and shadows do not talk and they certainly do not become detached from their owners, unless there is no light, then there can be no shadows."

"Have it your own way, but I am now refusing to talk to you because you say I am not an orphan shadow and I cannot talk, so there. And I might add, if I cannot talk then I cannot tell you about that strange man who has been following you about those silly things you are attempting to set up in the castle grounds, so there again!"

"We should not be too hard on the young lady as it must be very hard for her to accept we are here and can talk," replied the deeper voice. "Although I should say she is very lucky we have spoken to her as we normally keep very quiet when a person does find their way up here."

"Not that anybody has found their way up here for, I can't remember, it must be quite a number of years," added another voice from somewhere nearer the back of the attic.

"In the first place or even the second place, she is up in our retreat and we are only here because no-one ever comes here. What about if someone lights up all the oil lamps? In the darkness we cannot be seen, but if that happens, our shadows will be everywhere around the walls."

"I am very sorry to have disturbed you all, but I am looking for a basket of old clothes that I had been told was placed in the castle as it had been mistakenly brought here and stored until it could be collected. I have searched downstairs and could not find it, then I noticed this door and," but I was interrupted by a softer voice.

"And the young lady naturally came to see if her basket had been taken up here," said a softer voice that I thought must of a girl of similar age. "So you should all be sorry for having been so abrupt with her," the voice added.

"Archibald, what does the word 'abrupt' mean?" a voice asked.

"Abrupt? That means to be abrupt is to be abrupt. There is no other way of describing it."

"The young lady should go to the attic window and looks out. It is a little dusty and there are cobwebs are thick, but if you can clear a small part of it, you will see a person, a man, wearing a long black cloak with the hood upon his head. That is the person my fellow shadows spoke about. He has been following you since you arrived here."

Trying to think of an excuse to leave the room, I said, "thank you for telling me that and I am sure it is important. Perhaps I can find the baskets I am seeking elsewhere in the castle." Taking one last look through the gloom of the large open attic, I turned and made my way towards the door. Stopping, I looked back to see the shadows on the walls. There were many more there than I had first thought. Raising an arm, one began to wave to me, which I thought to be a nice gesture. Then others started to wave as slowly the light from the oil lamp dimmed and the black shadows against the black walls in a black room, became invisible.

Looking at the closed door and wondering how I would open it, it suddenly swung silently open as if expecting me. Walking slowly through and standing on the stone landing, I looked down the long spiral stairway. Nervous about treading on the first step, I waited awhile, then took the first step. Holding onto the rail with both hands, I again hesitated, expecting something strange to happen, but was relived when after a few moments, nothing did happen. Putting one foot slowly onto the lower step, then the next lower step, I again waited. Slowly, I stepped down a few more steps. Hoping the stairway would not spin around as it had before, I quickly skipped as fast as possible down the very many remaining steps until I once more found myself outside the small strange door. instantly swinging open, I walked through into the daylight as the sun brightly lit up the room.

Making a further unsuccessful search for the missing baskets and now satisfied they were not in the room, I made my way through the entrance door and out to the castle grounds, to see more small tents being erected and more seating set out. Keeping my head down, I wondered if the hooded man was still in the grounds or was perhaps close to me.

"You coming back with us?" a voice called out.

Seeing one of the circus assistants calling over to me, I answered 'yes' and made my way over to the waiting caravan, relieved to be going back to the circus and my caravan, still concerned about the missing baskets and the historic and sacred relic.

It was during lunchtime, that Carrie-Ann told me she would be accompanying her elderly father to a nearby town to discuss arrangements for the circus to move in a few weeks to a new site. It was only a few miles away and would remain there for the rest of the summer season. She also told me of an elderly clown, Tabalti, known as 'Professor Tabalti' once famous throughout the south coast. Now retired to a large house in nearby Christchurch. He and my father worked together since when they were both very young," she added. "He had a unique toy collection which he allowed visitors to view, I think, three days of the week. I do remember it included a number of teddy bears and ventriloquist dummies in addition to a number of historic items used in circuses during the last hundred years."

"I have not had any contact with him for a few years, but as we are here in Christchurch, if you have time, you might like to see if the collection can still be viewed," she suggested. "Visit him when you have an hour or two when you are not needed here and mention you are with our circus during the season and mention my father's name. If his collection is still available to view, I am sure he will be delighted to see you."

Thanking her, I finished lunch, wished her a pleasant journey and made my way back to our caravan to prepare me for the afternoon's performance when I would again enter the ring and lead the Shetland ponies around the arena. This time I would also have the responsibility of selecting the few children from the audience who would be chosen to ride the ponies around the ring.

The show opened as before with the complete ensemble making their way through the circus accompanied with the ringmaster very smartly leading them. Then the clown, conjurers and others each performed their acts to the delight of the youngish audience.

When it was over and the audience having left the marquee, like others, I gave a hand at helping arranging the chairs and whatever else needed to be done to make the marquee ready for the following day's performance. Making my way back towards the caravan and rested, I wondered about the visit to the clown's house. Being nearby and as there were a few hours before high tea, I would have plenty of time to visit the house.

Approaching the large distinguished house, I crossed the road and made for the front door, a few paces to the rear of a low iron railing fence. 'Professor Tabalti's Indoor Toy Collection', the sign on the door announced. The sign was faded and the leaves around the front door, with the paint peeling from the door, gave me the impression the door had not been used for some years. Above that was the notice, 'Tyneham House'.

Wondering if the collection was still available for viewing, I walked back a few paces to the pavement and noticed a narrow pathway to the side of the house. Following this, a short and narrow walkway led me to a side door, which was not as old as that on the front of the house and had obviously been used recently. Looking at the very strange looking chain to the side of the door, a notice announced, 'Pull me but not to hard'. I held out my hand and touched the handle at the end of the chain gently. A loud bell sounded and the door in front of me swung open. Before me was a small porch with a further door. After a few moments, that also opened to reveal an elderly man wearing dark jacket and trousers. Noticing how thin and very tall he was, he was bent almost double as he took a few steps towards me.

"Professor Tabalti?" I asked.

Scowling, he announced, "I am not. I am Jeremiah, the butler, bottle washer, door answerer and all other things unimaginable. What do you want?"

Slightly taken aback, I answered, "a friend in the nearby circus suggested I should take the opportunity to view the toy display and," but I had no time to finish as the man, scowling as if I was disturbing him in some way caused me to pause. Waiting a moment, I dared to ask, "is the toy display still available to be seen by members of the public?"

"The display closed and remains closed," he announced, seeming to make ready to close the door.

There was another silence making me wonder what else I could say. "I am assisting the local circus being held a short distance away for the summer months and I was advised to visited this house, I believe now owned by a famous former clown, Mr Tabalti, who was with the circus for many years and a friend of the owner. His daughter has asked me," but seeing the expression on the man's face, I suddenly stopped speaking.

"Professor Tabalti is not here at present being engaged in matters and will not be returning for some weeks hence." Looking at me, he continued scowling, then announced loudly, "very well, as you have been advised to view the collection by those who knew professor in his previous role whilst with that circus, you may come in provided you do not bring into this house any buttercups."

"Buttercups?" I asked, puzzled.

"Buttercups," he repeated, "they leave a strong odour causing me to sneeze," he said, standing back a short distance and allowing me to pass through the inner door.

"The notice on the front door does still mention visitors to this house may see a collection of old and antique toys," I reminded him.

"Of course, of course," he repeated. "However, you cannot see them until the fifteenth hour of the day. All the clocks in this house have stopped working and have not worked for many years, therefore I cannot know what the present time to be. Regrettably therefore you will have to await the fifteenth hour before commencing viewing any of the exhibits, despite your connection with Professor Tabalti, until I have been informed it is now the fifteenth hour of the day."

Disappointed, I asked, "are the clocks in the house broken?"

"Not broken, but have stopped working due to a house-keeper angrily taking all the keys to rewind the clocks, upon her dismissal from this house, many years ago and never returning them. However, as I have other things to do and do not want you waiting and disturbing me, I shall allow you to come in, despite the hour of the day. First must I make you aware this house is unlike others you may have visited in the past or will visit in the future. How many fingers do you have on your left hand?" he asked.

"On my left hand?" I repeated, somewhat surprised, "four fingers and one thumb."

"Five fingers, have you not?" he asked.

"Yes, five fingers," I answered, still puzzled.

"You should view the rooms in this house as you would view your left hand," he announced. "When I direct you to the first room of the displays, you will see before you on entering the first room, many forts and toy soldiers from the Kings Dragon guards, also a collection of toy soldiers from many other regiments and a table on which they are displayed as in a battle. When you are ready to see more exhibits in a further room, you will look towards the far wall, whereupon you will see two doors, allowing you to enter a further room, which will be the second room. Remembering you are using your left hand and are ready to journey to the second room, you should take the second from the left door, through which you will journey to the second room. Here you will see displays containing Victorian dolls houses, rocking horses from many Victorian houses from the past and dolls from generations past. As you pass from room to room, you should count upon the fingers of your left hand in which room you are leaving and into which room you will be entering."

"Count the fingers on my left hand?" I asked, somewhat puzzled.

"That is what I have taken great pains to make you aware. Only then will you know into which room you are about to enter and therefore which door you should open."

"I see," I replied, becoming confused. "But if I,"

"Should you lose count of which room you are presently in and enter the wrong door in your desire to access the next room, then you will be led you into a series of passageways whereby you will undoubtedly become lost. When you have seen all you wish to see and are ready to leave that second room, being eager to view the contents of the third room as I am sure you will, you should take note of the three doors on the far wall and go through only the third door from the left, ignoring the other two doors. You will then enter a room containing an exhibition of steam trains accompanied by mechanical toys."

He paused as if trying to regain his breath. "Should you then wish to enter the forth display room containing the famous collection of hand puppets, you will again notice towards the far wall, four doors. You will select the forth door from the left, ignoring the other three.

"All very simple, I am sure you will agree," he said, still scowling. "Whilst perusing the displays of glove puppets and marionettes in that room, please do not attempt to place upon either hand any glove puppet, even though a puppet may appear willing to be placed upon either of your hands. A number of glove puppets have complained to having been roughly placed over hands that are either too small or too cold."

Wondering what he meant, I asked, "and when I wish to enter the fifth room, having seen all I wish to see in the forth room, I assume I will see five doors in the far wall and take the fifth door from the left, but ignore the other four.

"Precisely, young lady. In the fifth room will you see a collection of

Professor Tabalti's ventriloquist dummies. I trust you will enjoy your visit and should any of the dummies wish to engage in conversation, please do not encourage them to talk too much or too loudly. Other smaller toys often become irritated by the loud speaking which they consider as loud and an unnecessary noise".

At this last statement, I tried to understand what he meant knowing ventriloquist dummies do not talk. "Should I become confused and take a wrong door," I asked, "will that door bring me back here?"

"The second door in the first room will bring you back here. The first door on the second room will bring you back here, but the third door in the second room will take you to an unmarked room which will then lead you back to the small landing on the first floor. From there you will make your way back the staircase to this, the ground floor."

"If there are five doors leading to the fifth room," I asked, "how will I leave that room to return here?"

"You should take the left door and take the narrow circular passage to leave the house by the back door. Please ensure you close it upon exiting and leaving this house."

"May I ask why there is such a strange arrangement of getting from one room to the next in this house?" I asked, not expecting an answer.

"Many years ago, this house was used to smuggle goods from the marshes. Such doors arrangements were used to confuse customs officers when conducting searches for illegal contraband." With that he pointed to a nearby door, where I noticed number one on the door and stomped off, leaving me concerned about making a mistake when leaving one room to enter another.

As I entered room number one, I held onto my thumb as I walked around the displays. Many toys were not in cabinets or on display as I had expected, but instead in groups as if thrown together. While the forts were stacked on top of each other and the lead soldiers were displayed on a large table, they appeared as if embracing each other rather than ready for battle. All displays were interesting, but I found myself looking towards the far wall for the two doors I had been told would lead me to the next room. Concerned, I could see no sign of any door as I approached the far wall, it was only when I came closer that the two doors suddenly appeared, from where I had no idea.

Remembering what I had been told and still holding the thumb on my left hand, I chose the second door from the left expecting to enter the second room. Standing in front of the door, I waited as nothing happened. Then, suddenly the door swung open to reveal a yellow coloured room. Walking quickly in as I was expecting the door to shut itself loudly behind me, I made my way into the room to see displayed, a number of tables of Victoria dolls houses, but the centre piece of the room was a very large rocking horse that was so high, I wondered how any child could ever ride it. What surprised me was how large the room was. I could not even see the far wall. Making an effort to now hold with my right hand, my thumb and first finger to remind me I was now in the second room. I spent only as much time as I thought I ought before nervously approaching the far wall, which took me a while to reach it, the room being so large.

Again there appeared to be no doors for me to use. Then as before, the doors appeared as if floating through the wall. Trying to remember that I was leaving the second room and entering the third room, I now held one thumb and two fingers of my left hand with my right hand. Entering a very small room with blue walls, I was surprised how small it was, but then noticed the display of steam trains and other mechanical tools which did not interest me too much. One train with carriages was presently travelling across the floor and almost ran over my foot. It was only when the train sounded it's horn that I quickly moved my foot out of the way, allowing it to speed quickly onwards. Many other train sets were placed on shelves in a jumble.

Walking around the far end of the last display I nervously looked towards the far wall. Then a large door appeared in the middle of the wall. Nervous, I could see only one door when I had expected to see four as I was about to enter the forth room. Then, relieved, one door appeared from the wall on one side of the main door, then two others appeared on the other side of the main door. Standing in front of the forth door from the left, which was a much smaller door than the main middle door that had first appeared, caused me to almost bend double to walk through it.

Entering the forth room and clutching one thumb and three fingers to remind me I was now in the forth room, I found myself gazing over shelves full of glove puppets. Remembering the butler had told me about not touching any of the puppets, I noticed many were looking directly at me as if almost begging me to place each one on my hand. Perhaps they missed times past when a slight movement by the puppet master would have an audience of children laughing at their continually changing expressions.

Now it was time to enter the fifth room and I was relieved to not having made any mistakes when choosing which door to enter the next room. The five doors this time all appeared together, even before I had time to reach the far wall. Carefully, I stood in front of the fifth door from the left, which then opened, allowing me to walk in.

Walking into a brightly lit room, I was sure I could hear voices. Waiting awhile, there was only silence. Continuing on, I passed rows of ventriloquist dummies hanging from hooks along one wall. All were dressed in distinctive costumes, with each smiling as if in front of an expectant audience. Looking more closely at a few, I came to one that was looking quite sad.

"Not smiling today," I said softly to myself, as there was no-one to listen to me.

"Alright for you, you can go home. Me! I am stuck here and have been here for so long, I can't remember when I first came here."

Stopping abruptly, I looked back to see if anyone had entered the room or was standing behind a display where they could not be seen. "We have been asked not to talk to the customers, you have not forgotten, I hope," called out another voice.

Now standing still in silence, I waited to see where the voice might be coming from.

"Betcha can't see who is talking"? asked a voice, as if challenging me.

"You are all ventriloquist dummies," I said loudly, although feeling a little silly. "Ventriloquist dummies do not talk!"

"Know that for a fact, do you, sunshine?" called out a voice, loudly.

"Can't talk? That's all you know," called out another from the far end of the row.

"Who is speaking to me, please can you tell me as I am becoming a little confused. Is there someone hiding behind the back of the displays?"

"It's me that has addressed your ladyship," called out a voice from the other end of the row. "Eugene is me name and how are you this fine day, if I might be so bold as to ask?"

"It was myself who also called out to you," added another voice. "Don't forget about those of us down this end of the row."

"I don't suppose there is any chance of you getting us out of here and back in front of an audience," added another deep voice.

"That's it, back on the stage, that is what I want. I was very popular on the stage at the end of the pier in Whitsable. People always came to see me on their holidays, Something to look forward to they always said," added a voice as other voices joined in.

"Dummies do not talk," I said loudly. "It has always been the ventriloquist who speaks for the dummy."

"Really? Try saying that when you are drinking a bottle of geer, I mean a bottle of beer."

Not understanding how any were managing to talk, I asked a question, but there appeared no answer. Perhaps I had been listening to recordings hidden away somewhere for the benefit of visitors. As I left to make my way to the far wall, I heard a voice call out, "bye then, come and see us all again soon. It can be boring talking to the same dummies all the time and having the same conversations. I mean, try getting an interesting or intelligent conversation out of a dummy!"

I stopped, hesitated, but then continued towards the wall hoping to see the doors appear. As two doors did appear, I tried to remember what I had been told about which door to use. Then as I was about to select the left door, two more doors suddenly appeared further along the wall. After a few moments, two further doors appeared on another wall, now there were six doors from which to chose.

Completely confused, I decided to push against the first door that had appeared. Easily opening, I could see only darkness ahead of me.

Wondering if I should walk on, a dim light suddenly lit up the area and I thought I must be walking into an attic with a very low roof. Taking a few steps forward, I noticed many beams supporting the roof and each other and I was reminded of my walk through the attic space of the Christchurch Priory as I tried to find my way out.

The way through seemed endless and I did wonder how much further I would have to walk. Then, thankfully I could just make out a wooden door with two small windows in the upper half, a short distance from me. As I approached, the small door instantly swung open and I could see a narrow gangplank connected to a large structure just outside the door. Making my way to the door, I was very surprised to see I was almost level with the top of a very high 'helter-skelter' funfair tower.

I had seen such towers in funfairs, where I would climb the stairs to the top and then getting a mat, use it to slide all the way down a slide connected around the structure. Perhaps, I thought, this has been used as a fun way to quickly get down to the ground, although who would use it, I had no idea.

Walking carefully across the narrow plank, I noticed a pile of mats at the top of the tower and close to the slide. Hesitating, I

"I slid around and around."

picked up one, placed it on the slide, sat of it and in an instant, I found myself sliding very fast around and around and around the giant tower until, with a thud, I slid onto the ground far below.

Picking myself up, I looked around and realised I was in the garden of the house I had been visiting. Making my way to the side of the house, I was again relieved to see the main road, where I could make my way across the fields and back to the circus.

The old courthouse.

Chapter Seven

Assisting at the circus, the Abbott
and a visit to the Priory Tower.

"Miss Jemima Jones, I do believe. I have been waiting for you for a few days. Why have you not been to see me before now?"

Looking down at the old lady sitting in her chair in front of a small tent, I was confused. "I am sorry," I said, as I stopped walking past a tent on the edge of the funfair. Looking at the old lady, I could only wonder how old she must be with her deeply lined and weathered face. Dressed in a long floral dress and with a coloured scarf covering most of her grey hair, which flowed down her back, she sat outside the entrance to her tent, scowling up at me.

"I am Madame Shavtof, the circus clairvoyant and Madame Shavtof does not have the time to wait forever. Time ages me. I must use what time I have left to carry out what I need to do. Time passes me now quicker than it has ever done. Therefore I ask, why have not been to see me before now?"

Complete confused about what the old woman was saying, I meekly replied, "no-one has told me you were waiting to see me."

"You and I must share a secret," she said, seeming to lower her voice and her sharp tone becoming more friendly. "There are those listening ears that do need to hear of those secrets. Come, my dear, we must seek the closed world we will find in my tent." At that, she with great difficulty managed to rise from her chair and with the aid of a stick, turned and struggled into the tent.

"Follow me," she commanded. "There are no prying eyes or listening ears to be found in my world inside my tent."

Following her into the tent, I became aware of how large it was inside. Moving towards the middle of the tent, the old lady sank down into a large armchair that almost hid her from my sight. Her colourful dress seemed to make her invisible and matched, almost completely, the pattern of the armchair.

"Now my dear, I am here to advise you. I am prepared to protect you and I am prepared to warn you of the danger you are in."

"Oh no, I am happy here and there is no danger from any of the animals as I have no contact with them except the Shetland ponies and they are so tame and friendly," I replied, I think not wanting to hear what she was about to say.

"Hush, girl. I speak not of dangerous animals, but of a dangerous human being. There is one who does even now seek you out and does even now follow you, that you might lead him to that which he desires more than anything else. That thing, that object, will allow that person to rule all he sees. It will allow that person to own all he desires. Take what I say to you lightly and that attitude will cause you the loss of your liberty. My message to you is of a serous nature and should be heeded."

"I am sorry," I replied, "and I do want to thank you for all you are saying as I believe you are trying to protect me." I paused, then continued, "I still cannot understand what it is or who it is that you think might be threatening me. The people I have met in my time with the circus are very friendly and very helpful."

"I speak not of any friends you might have made in the short time you have been with this circus. I have long been with this circus and am familiar with each and everyone here. No, I speak of one who comes from afar and comes into our midst to seek out a person of great importance and great humility. A person who has been selected by those of greater wisdom to be the keeper of a most sacred object and a person who in his distress has turned to you to assist him recover that which is so precious. It is an object that I myself have seen and have myself realised the importance of that item.

"When you say an important," but I did not have time to finish.

"Three performers at this circus did bring to me an object that they did think would bring to each of them financial gain should they sell it, if I perceived it to be of great value. Feeling the importance of the object, something I, nor others had ever seen before, I advised them it to be of little value and of little use. This had the desired effect of them not selling it, but then created a problem whereby they might throw it away and the important object become lost. Even with my long experience and clairvoyant powers, I was not able to see the reason for the object or how it had been, or was to be used. But I could feel the importance coming to me in a way I had not before known and could not understand."

"When I went to touch it, it moved away," I said.

"Quite so, quite so and now I come to the reason why I asked you here and scolded you because I have been awaiting you for so long."

"Yes," I said, feeling slightly nervous.

"My message to you is simple and it is this, beware. Beware of he who is about and who does pretend to be your friend. He has been to visit me and has sought what information I have on you. How he has decided you are the person who will lead him to that which he desires so much, I know not. My message to you, I repeat, is to beware, be alert and above all, pretend you do not know of his mission, when he shall again approach you. There is not more I can say, except this. You have sought the lost relic. I can tell you that your search has not been in vain. You were already very close to it, but did on that occasion miss it. It has since been placed into a larger case with another of similar size. Look for a large trunk which is covered in notices detailing many journeys around the world." She paused, then looking up at me said, "you may now leave me, I am old, I am tired and I must rest." With that the old lady seemed to slump further down into her chair and closed her eyes.

Looking at her for a few moments, I rose from the rickety chair where I had been sitting and quietly made my way towards the entrance of the tent, wondering about what I had been told and how I would proceed when the person mentioned, again approached me. Should I be nervous and show I was now aware of his mission or should I be friendly and avoid mentioning anything I know about the relic or the elderly Abbott, I had last seen in Christchurch priory? I also found myself again hearing the old lady saying, "placed into a larger case with another of similar size." I should now look for a large trunk covered in notices detailing many journeys around the world.

My attention was interrupted by a strong voice calling out to me, "my dear, I have been looking for you everywhere."

Looking around, the figure of Mrs hibbard came into view as she rushed towards me.

"Can't stop," she called out. "So many changes having to be made for the performance today. Jemima, could you please help us out by assisting the conjurer at the performance this afternoon? You don't have to appear in front of the audience, you will already be doing that when you lead the Shetlands around the ring, selecting two young visitors to ride the horses. No, perhaps you could help us later during the performance by helping the conjurer with the props he needs for his act. I have the details here somewhere," and she began to search the many pockets on the front of her dress. "I know I have the details somewhere," she said as both her hands hands searched various pockets. "Oh, here it is, I knew it would be somewhere. This is a list of the items he needs to be placed close to the ring and the order in which he needs them. Good luck." With that she flitted away as quickly as she had suddenly appeared.

The sight of so many circus workers and performers walking towards a large marquee near the edge of the site reminded me it was now close to lunchtime. Carrie-Ann had still not returned from her visit, so I would probably eat alone, although I was now making many new friends among the workers and performers that possibly today, seeing me alone, one or two might decide to join me.

With lunch over and many more new friends to greet, I wandered towards my caravan wondering about what the clairvoyant had said concerning the lost clothes basket. There was a possibility it had been taken to the arrangements still being made for the various displays at Priory House. As the Priory church was just a short walk away and the weather bright and sunny, I decided after a short rest and when my two tasks at the afternoon performance were complete, to make my way to the priory and again search for the missing basket. Perhaps when I returned later in the day, Carrie-Ann will have returned and I can catch up with her on her latest news.

While I found assisting the magician interesting, it was not something I would want to do regularity, I told myself after the performance had ended. Still, it was an emergency and the usual assistant would soon be returning to the circus. I was now left with a few hours to spare before high tea in which I could continue looking for the clothes basket containing the relic.

As I walked towards the priory church, looking up at the clock tower, I wandered into Castle street and made my way through the entrance to the graveyard and priory. Standing at the impressive entrance and looking up at the carved roof, I wondered why I found myself here and not on the lawn of Priory house.

On one side of the entrance, I noticed a small board with various notices listing various church events. One that caught my attention concerned the tower. Glancing at it, it detailed daily tours and individual access to the tower.

Walking on and pushing against one of the two heavy entrance doors, I began thinking how interesting it might be to see the surrounding town and countryside from the top of the tower. A helpful church warden explained I could climb the many steps to the top of the tower, but as there were already a number of people still awaiting to come down and the steps being so narrow, there would be a short delay.

Deciding instead to wander around the interior of the large church, I made my way to the near wall and wandered along the aisle, looking at the many inscriptions on the walls and the small chapels dedicated to past saints and others. Continuing on, I made my way past the place where the 'miraculous beam' was placed, high above my head and a subject if great interest to a number of visitors all struggling to read the notes about the history of the beam. Now at one end of the church, I began to make my way along the far aisle and past the steps leading up towards the high altar.

Looking up at the carvings over the altar, I thought I could hear my name being whispered quite close to me. Looking around and wondering who could know my name, I could see no-one near me. Looking again up at the altar, I was surprised to see all the visitors who had been inspecting the various monuments and items of interest close to me had now disappeared. I seemed to be alone as if the church had suddenly closed. Again I thought I heard my name being whispered. Looking about me, I again looked up towards the high altar and then found myself looking down, noticing in the wall supporting the altar, a small door, opening slowly as I looked at it. Again, I could hear my name being called, this time a little louder.

Not being sure if I should walk away or more closely to the door, I found myself bending slightly to see what lay beyond the door and saw a series of stone steps leading downwards. Hesitating, I waited, then a soft voice called out, "Jemima, walk down the steps, I await you."

Not really knowing why, I carefully made my way down the steps, until I found myself as I reached the final step, in a dimly lit but large room.

"Where am I?" I heard myself ask.

"You are here with me under the high altar," answered a voice from within the gloom.

Looking towards the far wall, I could just see a few caskets lying in the far wall, causing me to immediately step away.

"Fear not my child, you are with me," called out the soft voice, again as if not wanting to be overheard.

Looking around I still could not see any other person in the room and wondered if I should instead quickly walk away and nearer the steps.

"There is no-one here," I called out, still looking around in the gloom.

"I am here and I have been here since last we met in St Michael's Loft. You recall?" the voice asked.

As if appearing through the wall, the figure of the elderly Abbott suddenly appeared, causing me to almost turn and run up the stairs.

"You gave me such a shock," I exclaimed, my heart beating.

"I am here and here shall I stay where I am safe," the figure replied, then seeming to sit on a stool, which I had also not seen.

"You were in that room very high in the church," I said," trying to think of what else I could say. Then added nervously, "the one with the window."

"Indeed I was, my aging bones have allowed me to come down from that high loft, but do not allow me to again climb those many steps. Now my child, you will of course not divulge my presence here to a living soul, even if that soul shall worship none but himself and those who do now follow him in the hope of gain."

"Sir, I was warned that a person, a man has been following me since last we met."

"Be not too troubled, my child. He seeks information and will harm you not. Indeed, his time is running out and if he is not successful in finding me and where I am to transfer my responsibly, his mission and his followers are finished. Go now and continue your tour and other arrangements you have made. The time I have awaited is nearing and I will come to you again. Soon, your mission and your assistance will be ended. Go now and be troubled not."

There was a noise behind me as I heard the door above open. Feeling a slight breeze flow into the room, I turned back to say goodbye, but the Abbott was gone and the room now empty and gloomy. Shivering at the cold air as it surrounded me, I made my way up the stone steps and into the aisle. Stepping out, I felt another rush of air as the small door closed quickly behind me. Stopping for a moment and wondering what to do, I became aware of many voices around me. Looking around, I found myself surrounded by a party of visitors, brushing past me as a speaker described to them the many items of interest along the aisle.

Wandering slowly past the many visitors, but hardly noticing any of them, I again heard someone calling to me, but this time in a very different voice. "Young lady, if you still wish to climb to the top of the tower, all other visitors have now left. Please be careful and take extra care with the narrow steps when you descend. You will find the bell tower to be the main room of interest as you go up."

Thanking the lady, I made my towards the first of the many steps I would have to climb, thinking of the many generations who had climbed these same steps since they were first built, hundreds of years ago.

The first room I discovered was a large room with the colourful ends of a number of ropes hanging from large holes in the ceiling. Each was placed neatly against the far wall. This, I supposed was where the bell ringers would ring their bells each Sunday and on other occasions. Continuing on, I began to climb the steps to the next floor.

Here, I was very surprised to find myself gazing over a number of large bells. Thinking to count the bells, I managed to count twelve and looked at the timbers and steel fastenings used to secure them in their positions.

Looking towards the ceiling, I noticed the louvered windows in the tower walls allowing the bells to sound out across the surrounding town and countryside and I supposed, the cold winds, sweeping across the marshes on a winter's evening, to enter and sweep into the tower.

The priory bell room.

"Regards, mi-lady, you come to inspect my bells, have you?" called a voice from somewhere across the other side of the room.

Looking over towards the wall, I could not see anyone, then the voice called out again, "bet you can't see where I am hiding."

Suddenly a smallish man, wearing a dark overall and with a tall pointed hat upon his head, appeared behind one of the larger pieces of timber.

"Bet you didn't expect to find me here, did you, mi-lady? Sometimes I hide here when I hear people come into my bell room and then I thinks to myself whether I want to talk to them or not. Depends on how I feel. Sometime I do and sometimes I do not. Have you by any chance brought with you any lettuce and cucumber sandwiches?"

Surprised by the question, I simply answered, "I am afraid I have not," it was all I could think to say, still looking at this strange small figure.

"I am very partial to lettuce and cucumber sandwiches so that is disappointing. No matter, you are still welcome to my bell room." Looking at me, he continued, "did you notice, when you was looking around my bell room, how tidy it is and how everything is in it's place?"

"Oh yes," I said, thinking I should say something nice and then quickly continue upto the top of the tower.

"Normally, if I decide to talk to people about the bells in my bell room, I tells them of how the tower contains a ring of 12 bells, plus a flat 6th semi-tone bell, dating from the end of the 14th century to 1976. The two oldest, two of the oldest in England still in use, were cast in 1370 by a John Rufford of Bedfordshire, who was appointed the Royal Bell founder by King Edward III in 1367," he paused, then added, "but I suppose you already knew that, so I don't have to bother explaining it to you. While you are here is there anything else you would like to know?"

Unprepared for the question, I replied, "are you always here, I mean, is there anyone to help you keep the bells and this room neat and tidy?"

"Now that is the question no-one has asked before. Always rushing upto the top, they are. Never interested enough to ask how I am. No-one asks Talisman, the bell man at the top of the tower, how he is."

"Talisman, that is an interesting name," I replied, feeling now a little more relaxed.

"And an interesting job I have here if people would only stop to listen to the hours and work I put in keeping this place shipshape, you might say. And, I keeps my mouth shut when I am repairing late at night, the sights I sees when looking out over those marshes. Don't tell no-body, I don't. Only concerned about keeping my bell room in good working order. That way, when them what's down below in front of the vicar with their families and all them guests, it's me Talisman, who makes all bells sound loud and clear across the countryside."

"That is very nice of you, but you didn't say if anyone helps you."

"Helps me? No-one would know how to help me. There's the oiling of the joints, the inspections of the ropes. Them what be downstairs pulling at the ropes, don't think about how the ropes might feel as they are pulled up and down over all the weeks of the year. Talisman does all that, that's who. Then there is the other side of my work."

"Your other side?" I asked.

"What is it you first see when you approach this tower?" he asked, looking at me with a slight smile on his face.

 Thinking about the question, I replied, "I see the stonework on top of the tower."

"No, you see the clock," he burst out. "You see a clock and when you see the tower from different directions, you see the same time on each clock and who makes that all possible, I hear you ask?"

"Talisman," we both replied together.

"Of course, Talisman, him what keeps everything shipshape. There was one occasion, when I was much younger of course, when folks hereabouts complained the hands on the clock were going the wrong way around the clock face." The vicar climbed up the stairs and said, "the clock was not working as it should be. Kindly put it right."

"I replied that was impossible because only that morning I had cleaned, oiled and adjusted the mechanism myself."

"Were the hands going the wrong way?" I asked, hoping the question would not to annoy the strange man, who now seemed to be friendlier.

"Unfortunately, I had adjusted the clock and done all necessary things that should have been done and then stood back to see the clock face fully working. I had forgotten that I was looking at the back of the clock. The face on the other side was opposite to the one I was looking at. I had arranged the hands to go clockwise as I looked at the clock, but the hands went anti-clockwise for those looking at the clock from outside the tower."

"It has been a pleasant experience talking to you and learning of all the things you do and I suppose continue doing at all hours of the day."

"All hours of the day," he repeated. "That is correct."

"Now I must be on my way to see the wonderful views from the tower top," I said beginning to make my way out of the room.

"Wonderful views indeed, mi-lady. I sometimes stay up there to see the sun arising over the Isle of Wight first thing in the morning and when the last part of the day is upon us and the sun gradually sinks below the horizon and dusk slowly sweeps across the marshes until it covers all. But, you must look about you. That is what I would advise, mi-lady. Look about you."

"I am not sure what you mean," I said, now very close to the opening leading to the stairs.

"There has recently been a large bird, a large ugly bird that has swept in from no-where and settled itself upon the wall on many an occasion. There it has stayed and looked downward. So often has it looked downward, that I have the conclusion it does seek something or someone. Then suddenly, it will flap it's giant wings and swoop away."

"A large bird," I asked, "and it just sits there?"

"Sits there it does, mi-lady. A buzzard, the largest ever I did see and gazing across the marshes from the tower top. I have seen many large birds as I have looked across the marshes these many years, but none so large as that one."

"Have a care, mi-lady, have a care." With that, he suddenly disappeared behind one of the wheels next to the furthest bell.

Waiting a few moments in case he should reappear, I turned and continued up the stone stairway. Reaching the top and slightly out of breath, I was delighted to see the sun shining. At last I was at the very top of the tower.

Looking first down over the graveyard to the entrance to the church, I tried to identify the few buildings I was familiar and then walked to the other side and looked over the marshes and harbour.

Almost spellbound, I visited each of the four walls, spending a little time seeing all I could see.

There, far below me was the old castle keep. Long since ruined at the same time the monks were forced to leave their priory. I then became aware of a dark cloud sweeping across the sky.

Looking up, I was disturbed to see the wings of a large bird, hovering a short distance above my head. Flapping it's wings, the air about me became as a fierce wind and I instantly bent down to avoid it crashing down on my head.

Seeing to my side the small entrance to the rooftop, I dashed across the roof, still keeping very low and quickly made my way into the shelter of the door. Making my down a few steps and feeling safe, I looked back to

see the large buzzard perched on one of the corner stones and looking intently down at the ground far, far below. Waiting a little longer, it flew off and I continued making my way down the steps. Leaving the priory entrance, I waited and looking around, thought the bird now gone. I quickly made my way back to the circus and my friends.

Chapter Eight

Meeting again the Richards twins
and a trip to Mudeford.

Wondering where I would first visit, Carrie-Ann had now returned and I wanted to see her, but there were a few other things I had to do. Time, I thought, to start making out lists as does Mrs Hibbard, Also, I had been told that lady wished to see me concerning one of the Shetland ponies.

Wondering which task to start first, I suddenly felt there might be someone standing just behind me. As I turned, a voice called out, "bet you be thinking, there's two strange men standing just behind you and smiling at you. Did you think the young lady is thinking the same thing, did you, brother Richard?"

"Indeed I did, brother Richard, indeed I did. Shall we remind the young lady who we are? Perhaps the young lady has forgotten us since that time. Do you think she has, brother Richard?"

"Now that you mention it, brother Richard, I think your suggestion to remind this young lady of our name is timely."

"Timely?" replied the second person. "Yes, considering the circumstances, I believe the word 'timely' to be the correct word to be used on this occasion."

"Do you really, brother Richard, sometimes I think you are so clever."

"If you think I must be clever, then you also must be clever, because we are twins."

As the two persons seemed to be talking to each other and forgotten about me, I said, "I do indeed remember you. You are both named Richard, although I seem to remember that you both like to do sensible things and I also remember that sometimes on formal occasions, one of you becomes Richard One on weekdays."

"And on those occasions, I become Richard One on weekends," interrupted the other.

"Well done," said one, "and we do remember your name, don't we brother Richard?"

"Of course, of course," added the other man. "We both remember your name is, is." He turned to his brother. "The young lady's name is?"

"My name is Jemima," I quickly said, "Jemima Jones."

"Of course, of course. That is the very name I was just about to say. Indeed it was on the tip of my tongue," added one Richard.

"The tip of your tongue, how brilliant of you, brother Richard, but we have not asked the young lady, who's name we all know is Miss Jemima Jones, about what she is about?"

"About what she is about?" added the other Richard. "What is about what is she about, supposed to mean?"

"I mean, how the young lady is getting on now she is one of us, how is she enjoying her time with the circus?"

"Amazing brother Richard, I was just about to ask the young lady that very same question. I am sure we are both eager to know the answer to that question. Are we both in agreement on that matter, brother Richard?"

"Perfect agreement, my dear brother, perfect agreement."

"Miss Jemima Jones, how are?" Turning to his brother, he asked, "what was the question I am supposed to ask?"

Realising this conversation could go on for a long time, I interrupted both of them. "I am very happy here and I have been getting more varied tasks and learning more about the circus."

"That is wonderful, isn't that wonderful, brother Richard. Did you just hear what the young lady said?"

"I did indeed hear what the young lady has just said because I am, at this very moment, standing next to you," replied the brother, scornfully.

"Of course you are, of course you are," agreed the other Richard.

"I do remember the last time we met, do you also remember that time, brother Richard?"

"That was the first time we met," interrupted the other Richard.

"All right, clever clogs. The other time we met was also the first time we met and the young lady was looking for something," he said, turning his attention back to me.

"We do indeed. I also remember that silly monkey had taken an item to the top of the circus marquee and left it up in all those ropes.

"Oh no, brother Richard, that was old news. The new news was that the monkey later brought it down again. Do you not remember?"

"Now that you mention it, I do remember the new news overrode the old news. So the new news is what we should be remembering," added one Richard,

Now completely confused and wanting to be on my way, I said, "I am very pleased to see you both again and yes I am still looking for that item. I have been told it might be stored in a large trunk with many labels showing the many places the trunk has travelled over the past years."

"Travelled over the past years with many labels showing the many places the trunk has travelled. Well fancy that brother Richard, just like our great grandfather's trunk."

"Great grandfather's trunk, indeed," replied the other Richard.

"You have a trunk like that?" I asked, becoming just a little excited. "May I ask where it is?"

"Will I tell her or will you tell her, brother Richard?"

"Oh stuff and nonsense, you can't even do a simple task. Tell the young lady where is great grandfather's trunk."

"Very well, if you think I am the best person to tell her. Our great grandfather's trunk is very large and is often used to store many smaller baskets, when they need to be taken somewhere. Did I say that correctly, brother Richard?"

"Very correctly, very correctly, indeed," was the reply, "but you did not tell the young lady where the trunk now is."

"Is it somewhere nearby?" I asked.

"Very near, very near indeed. No, actually it is not near, is it brother Richard? It is outside the props tent and due to be taken by open wagon to, I believe the village is named Mudeford. There are a number of funfair attractions beings set up on the village green for the next few weeks of the school holidays. Is it not so, brother Richard?"

"Indeed indeed," replied the other brother. "A display is due to be erected there and what fun it will be. I might even want to go on a few of the rides myself."

At that moment I thanked them both and quickly made my way towards the props tent.

"The lady seems to have left us, brother Richard."

"So it seems, so it seems," replied the other Richard and together they went on their way chattering about this and about that, which was probably of no interest whatsoever to anyone else.

Making my way quickly towards the props tent, I was dismayed to see a large number of bags and equipment being loaded onto a large wagon. Seeing the very large trunk I was seeking quite close to the end of the baggage, I was pleased to see it was covered in travel labels, so knew my search had not been in vain. Approaching it and wondering how to open the many catches, a man seeing me, came towards me.

"Too late to do anything with that one, young lady, we are just about to load it."

"I am with the circus," I said, thinking I should make myself known.

"Know that already," the man replied, "seen you in the ring with those

Shetland ponies."

Going over and pulling the trunk onto the back of the wagon, he turned then called over to me, "you going with us then, better be quick we are already late, need to have this lot delivered by late morning and the items set out ready for assembling."

"Er, yes," I said, thinking very quickly.

"Well then, be quick and hop up. Make yourself comfortable as you are able, it's a nice trip. The girl is going with us," he called out to the driver of the wagon. "Doing something with the large labelled trunk, she is." he said as he left me and walked quickly towards the front of the cart, climbing up and joining the driver.

Quickly climbing onto the rear of the open wagon, I began to feel a jolt as the wagon moved reluctantly under the heavy load. Looking for somewhere to sit, I held onto the sides as the wagon as it lurched this way and that.

The voyage through the old village of Stanpit and towards Mudeford was interesting as between the old cottages, I could just make out glimpses of the Stanpit marshes and the waters of Christchurch harbour. The journey did not take too long, but I was pleased when finally we came within sight of the entrance to Mudeford Quay. To my right, I could now see a clearer view of the marshes and the small island, almost submerged in the waters. Ahead of me were a number of old cottages and beyond them, looming up, I could distinctly see, the forested area known as Hengistbury Head.

"We'll stop here and unload," called out a strong voice from the front of the wagon. "Keep clear as we unload, Missy, we wouldn't want to have any accidents or we'll never hear the end of it from Mrs Hibbard." Glad to be alighting from the wagon, I jumped down onto the grass and walked over to one of the many benches, waiting for my chance to examine the trunk once it and other baggage had been off loaded.

Once most of the heavier displays and other items were laid out on the grass ready for sorting and assembly, I made my way over to the large trunk. Being on the edge of most of the other baggage, meant I could easily make my way to it. There were, I noticed, a large number of catches securing the lid to the trunk, but finding all of them, I was able to open the lid to see four smaller baskets placed neatly together. With a slight leap in my heart, I was quickly able to identify the one I had first seen in the caravan I shared with Carrie-Ann.

"Help you with those, miss?" called out a voice behind me.

Without any time for me to reply, the man was already pulling one of the baskets out of the trunk. Seizing two more, one in each hand, he easily lifted each out and placed them on the grass. As he reached into grasp the one I had been seeking, he let out a gasp. "Cor," he exclaimed, "this one is really heavy, can't even move it." Calling out to his colleague, he called, "ere, Harry, give me a hand with this one, don't know how anyone managed to lift it in here in the first place."

Coming to join him, the other man, looked into the trunk and remarked, "what's the problem? Never had no bother lifting that one in. Did it myself, if I'm not mistaken."

"Well, try lifting it out then," called out the first man.

Standing closer, the man rubbed his hands together and grasped the top of the basket and gave a pull. "Won't budge," he called out. "Can't make it out. I'm sure this was the one I put into the trunk this morning."

"Let's leave it and we'll sort out the other stuff first," advised the first man, "otherwise we are going to be behind in getting the other stuff assembled."

"Can't help you just yet, young lady," one said looking at me. "We'll get on with the other gear and deal with this problem later."

With that, they both left with me calling, "thank you anyway."

It was after they had been gone a few minutes and were now busy sorting out the rest of the equipment that I thought I might try to see if the relic was still safe in where I had left it. Removing the lid was easy enough. Pulling aside the few towels and similar items, I was pleased to note nothing seemed to have been disturbed since I had hidden the item in the basket. Feeling deeper, I was overjoyed to feel my fingers touching the strange object. Then I wondered if I would be able to move it or would it be too heavy for me to move.

Slowly I pushed my fingers below the relic and bringing my hand up, was so relieved to feel the relic move with my hand. Pausing awhile, I waited, then lifted my hand a little higher until the relic was clear of the basket, but still hidden by the sides of the trunk. Thinking about what the circus clairvoyant had warned me, I wondered how best to hide the relic. Selecting a few towels from the basket, I carefully wrapped these around it, holding it close to me. Then, again looking around, made my way towards the two men who had tried to help me. "It is alright," I called out. "I have what I wanted. The basket only contains laundry items and has been sent here by mistake, so can be returned."

"OK Missy," one called out, "we'll put it to one side, will you return with us or make your own way back to the circus?"

Thinking about what was being said, I quickly thought and then said, "I am not sure, you will be here for sometime and as I now know the way." "Fair enough," was the reply with both men seeming relieved, then getting on with their work.

Making my way towards the far end of the narrow piece of land jutting out into the harbour, I stopped where the waters from the harbour rushed out to meet the sea. As a few fishermen prepared their nets and baskets, I watched as across the water, one fisherman cast his net, hoping to catch the fish, caught up in the fast flowing water.

Early morning fishing.

Walking along the edge of the quay, I waited, then selected a nearby bench to relax and watch the visitors as they explored the quay and surrounding area.

"Day dreaming, young lady?" a voice brought me out of my thoughts. "Nice place to relax, first visit here, is it?"

Looking down I noticed a fisherman just climbing up the steps to the quay from a small fishing boat.

"Er, no," I replied, wondering if I should say anything more.

Then he asked, "just visiting?"

"There is a small funfair being setup on the green and I have travelled here with some people, but will soon need to make my way back," I replied.

"Oh, with the circus are you? That must be exciting. That must be the one near Stanpit marshes, thinking of taking my children there myself."

"I must think about walking back," I said, starting to get up.

"What back to Stanpit marsh, you be walking?" he asked.

"Yes," I replied, "I will be taking the same way back that the wagon brought me here."

"You'll be wanting to go to Christchurch Quay, then, that be closer to the circus than Stanpit marsh. Give you a lift if you want, I'm off to Tuckton, be passing the quay in Christchurch on my way."

"Er," I said, not knowing whether to accept this stranger's invitation.

"Just give me a couple of minutes to drop of some stuff to my family home over there and I will be right back."

Watching him go, I noticed he walked quickly over to the low house on the edge the quay,

It was a few minutes later, as he had said, that he emerged.

"Right", he said, "I'll climb down into the boat and then help you down these steps."

Still not sure if I should accept the invitation, I found myself getting up and following him.

"My name is Jemima," I said, thinking I should say something. "Jemima Jones."

"Just call me Bill," he replied. "It's William Foster, but I have been here all my life, so everyone here just refers to me as Bill."

As I sat in the front of the boat with my companion sitting next to the engine in the rear, I felt a sense of excitement as finding myself almost level with the surface of the water. I waited for the small craft to move.

With the engine suddenly chugging and the boat starting to move away from the quay, I looked ahead at the wide panorama from the Mudeford spit with it's many beach huts, to the wide expanse of the harbour.

"That's my house, there," he called out. "Been in the family since I don't know when, my mother still lives there as well as my family."

"Very attractive house," I called out as we passed almost under it.

"Nice in the summer, but can be a problem with the wind and tides in the winter months," he replied. "Usually have to use sandbags to keep the water out. Very handy for work, though."

Again I relaxed in the front as gently we glided across the vast expanse of water on our way to the distant quay.

"Two rivers flow into this harbour," he called out. "The Avon and the Stour. They join together not far from here. That black house we just passed was used by smugglers in the past."

Content just to watch the passing scenery with the continuous reed beds to one side of me and the flat open plains of the marshes to my right, I began to hope the short journey would last longer.

'Black House' - often used by smugglers.

"Taking a parcel to someone?" he asked.

"Er, no," I nervously said, clutching the towels containing the relic closer to me. "Just returning an unused item back to the circus."

As we journeyed on, passing the looming Christchurch Priory, the fisherman called out, "next stop Christchurch Quay. From there you just walk past the old watermill, past the priory and then a short distance to where the circus is being held."

"Yes," I called out. "I know my way from the priory," as the small craft slowed it's speed and drifted gently towards a few stone steps not far from what I could see must be the old watermill.

"Take care with the steps, they can sometimes be slippery," he called out, as I stood up in the boat trying to balance myself and walk towards the steps.

Having managed that, I turned, waved and called out to thank him. "Come and see the circus soon," I said.

Smiling, he turned the boat and continued on in the direction he had been going.

Now on my own and with the easy task of finding my way back to the circus I selected a nearby bench. Sitting down, I thought about what I should do to ensure the safety of the relic. I could not walk through the priory looking for the older Abbott and I did not know enough places in the circus where I might again hide the object. Instead, I thought I should look for a hiding place nearby where I could be confident it would not be found until I could retrieve it before handing to the Abbott.

Making my way towards the narrow entrance to the pathway, following the side of the priory, I was dismayed to see in the distance the figure of the younger Abbott, now I remember a

The old watermill.

friar or monk. He seemed to be standing very still as if looking for someone or something, near the entrance to the graveyard. Quickly turning back as he had not yet seen me, I made my way towards the old mill I had just passed, desperately trying to think what to do. Without anywhere to go, I found myself walking into the mill, making my way up the rickety wooden steps to the upper floor. Looking for a window, in case I should be able to see if the person would be coming towards me, I waited patiently, not really knowing what else I could do. I also realised that if he had seen me and decided to come this way, I would have no means of escape if he should decide to inspect the interior of the mill.

Walking around the exhibits in an attempt to calm myself and think what else I could do, I stayed as long as I could near the window. Then a call came from downstairs, "be closing in ten minutes, love, early closing today."

"Thank you," I called down making my way slowly to the top of the stairs. Taking a few steps down, pausing then again searching the lower floor for any sign of the friar, I quickly came down the remaining stairs and waited by the main door before walking out of the building. "Be open again, nine in the morning," the helpful assistant called out.

"Thank you," I again said and walked slowly out of the door quickly looking for somewhere I could hide myself until I was sure it was safe for me to continue on. Thinking about how I would make my way back to the circus, I remembered Carrie-Ann had pointed to an old bridge that led to a path following a stream dug by the monks, centuries ago. 'That is another way back,' she had told me.

Turning to my right, I quickly crossed over the small humped bridge and followed the stream around until I was at the main road, not far from Tyneham house, where I had visited the old clown's toy exhibition. Turning right and following the road, I decided when I approached the part where I would normally walk towards the recreation ground, to instead continue on and follow another path that would lead me a longer way to the recreation ground.

Finally and continually looking around me, I was back at the circus and relaxed slightly, but still could not think where to safely secure the important relic without anyone finding it. Seeing one of the circus horses being led back to the stables reminded me that there were a number of large baskets storing grain for the Shetland ponies for the season. Making my way towards that part of the grounds, I was soon outside the makeshift stables to house the ponies.

Walking to the back of the storage area, I selected the last container, forced off the lid and emptied much of the grain as I was able on a nearby table, placed the relic, still wrapped in the towels, into the grain and refilled the rest of the grain into the basket. Securing the lid, I then walked back to the caravan to be greeted by the ever friendly Carrie-Ann. I had lots to tell her about my additional circus tasks and about the old clowns strange toy collection.

Walking past the quaint shops leading to the Priory Church.

Chapter Nine

A strange meeting with a strange person.

First task after breakfast I told myself, was to ensure the baskets of grain for the ponies were where I had left them. Making my excuse to Carrie-Ann that I needed to check on the Shetland ponies before talking them out for exercise later in the morning, I said I thought the food stocks might be getting a little low.

"That might be a bit inconvenient this morning," she replied. "The horses and ponies are being rehoused this morning in a different area. Some of the circus staff are already making the necessary changes. Might be better if you visited the stable later so as not to get in the way, I know they all started first thing this morning, so may well finish soon."

Thanking her for the information, I could feel a nervousness in my stomach as I imagined losing the relic for a second time. Saying I might instead go for a short stroll, I left the caravan and quickly made my way to where I had previously left the relic.

Entering the tented area, I was dismayed as I saw the ponies and all baskets of food supplies now missing, along with all other items, such as the saddles and the bedding straw. Seeing one of the helpers I thought might be involved in the work, I quickly ran after him, asking if he could let me have any details of what arrangements had been made.

"They were probably going to let you know once all the work had been finished," he said. "Means you may have to exercise the ponies later in

137

the morning."

"But where are they?" I insisted.

"Further away from the public," he replied, "nearer the hedge running alongside the old path leading to the Stanpit marsh visitor centre."

Thanking him, I quickly made my way there and was pleased to see the ponies and horses now together and in a larger roped-off area. Seeing the newly erected tents behind them, I made my way to each in turn. It was only when I got to the last one that I could see the collection of baskets of grain and other things needed for the welfare of both horses and ponies had been stored together. My relief turned to alarm when I realised similar baskets had been used for almost everything. Counting at least twenty baskets and there were probably some I could not see, I wondered how I could go about the enormous task of finding the one in which I had hidden the relic.

As I was about to walk closer to the nearest basket, a voice called out behind me, "so you found our new arrangement. The horses and ponies, you can see will not have to travel so far to enter the ring and both are closer to the marshes for their morning exercise walk and further away from the noise of the funfair events."

Turning around, there was Carrie-Ann in her wheelchair smiling up at me. "Nice improvement, I think you'll agree?" she said.

"Yes, yes," I replied, still thinking how soon would I be able to begin my search of the newly moved baskets.

"Now," she continued, "I have some exciting news for you. News I think you will find agreeable. A few of us have been invited to travel to Salisbury to talk to another circus company about arrangements for the season next year. There are things we might share and things we will each do alone. I thought you might like to accompany us to that town and while we are talking circus talk, thinking about ideas for next year's season, you might like to take the opportunity to explore the historic town of Salisbury and perhaps the cathedral."

Mumbling as I could see my opportunity to search for the relic fading away, but felt I could not refuse the generous offer.

"Thank you very much," I said, "I am sure I will enjoy the visit," disappointed the visit would be today.

"As there will be no performance today, we will not have to rush there or back again. We have our own vehicle we use for such purposes, so you will be very comfortable."

"Thank you again," I replied.

"We can leave after you have exercised the ponies and have rested yourself. You don't need to bring anything, perhaps a raincoat."

The long trip to the town of Salisbury was interesting as we passed old villages and lovely scenery. Many times I caught glimpses of the river Avon as it flowed towards Christchurch village, where I knew it would then make it's way out to sea after reaching Christchurch harbour. Finally as we came over a hill, we looked across the valley to see the tall steeple rising high over the cathedral. Journeying on, we travelled the short distance into the town and past centuries old walls, surrounding the cathedral.

As the journey ended and we prepared to leave the vehicle. I stayed behind to assist Carrie-Ann with her wheelchair. Arranging a time when we would all meet, I was shown the direction towards the historic market square while the others in the party went on foot to their arranged meeting place.

Now left alone, I looked around me wondering where best to start my exploring this old town. The market square seemed the best place to start, as I had been told it was in the popular centre of the town's activities.

Although I enjoyed seeing the many old and varied shops, I found myself still thinking about the relic hidden in the grain basket, concerned that perhaps that would be the very basket selected by someone to feed the animals and the relic discovered and perhaps discarded.

Finding myself at the beginning of a narrow but attractive alleyway, I noticed at the far end a very old stone gatehouse. I assumed it to be the entrance to a castle or something equally old. What I did find interesting was the very large coat of arms over the open gateway. Making my way towards it and then through it, I saw before me a series of very old and very quaint houses either side of the narrow passageway. Walking on slowly and admiring the structures and decorations on the houses, I came to a large open green area, surrounded by many large and very impressive houses. Fascinated by the decorations on the various houses, I followed the visitors in front of me, until I found myself looking up at the cathedral, towering over the surrounding houses and fronted by a rich green lawn.

Fascinated by the size of the building, it's carved stone statues and the tall steeple, seeming to reach so high into the sky, I made my way slowly towards it, trying to see all the decorations and sculptured figures as I became nearer.

Inside, I found an awe inspiring interior, but also a little gloomy. Making my way towards the main part of the interior, I noticed a shortish man quickly walking over and approaching me. Dressed in a long black cloak and holding out his hand he said, "good day, Miss, we have been expecting you. It is seven minutes past the hour so you are not too late for your appointment. I am pleased to take you to another of my colleagues." With that he simply let go my hand, turned and walked away without any further explanation.

"This way," he called out as he seemed to be counting the steps he took.

Thinking he must be mistaking me for someone else, I was about to call to him, but first I would need to catch up with him.

Stopping suddenly, he said, "I am a short person so cannot go any further, a person who is six inches taller than myself will be very happy to take you further. I do hope you will enjoy your visit with us." He then walked away and disappeared into one of the small chapels without a further word.

"Good day, Miss Jemima," a voice said, as I was still looking at the chapel where the small man had just disappeared. Turning, I saw a similarly dressed man approach me, smile and say, "I am six inches taller than your last guide so am able to take you a further short distance where we will reach the edge of the main hall. Please to follow." Turning and without any explanation, he seemed to want to lead me further into the interior of this vast church. Not knowing whether to follow or simply walk away and explore the cathedral by myself, I thought best to follow and ask how he knew my name and why he thought he should lead me somewhere.

Reaching where the columns ended, the guide stopped, saying "we are here and I am unable to go any further. A new guide who will be six inches taller than myself is qualified to take you further. You will be expected." Without a further word, he simply walked away towards the wall of the church, opened a small door in the wall and crouching down, disappeared inside.

Completely confused by these strange guides, I then became aware of another person approaching me. "Just a short distance towards the chapel," he said, "where another guide, six inches taller than myself will direct you to His Excellency." Turning and saying little else, he walked on. Struggling to catch up with him, I tried to say something, but he appeared not to hear me. Eventually he came to a stop so I had the chance to quickly ask, "why does everyone keep talking about being six inches taller?"

"The taller one is Miss, the further one can travel into this cathedral. The shortest persons must start at the main door and proceed only as far as their height allows, which is a full sixty paces."

I was about to say that seemed to me to be very silly, when he added, "each person you will see from the first you did see, will be six inches taller than the previous person. If a person should grow a further six inches, then he will become qualified to walk sixty further paces into the interior of this cathedral in addition to the sixty paces his height already allows."

"Supposing a person does not grow another six inches and has reached the final height he will ever grow?" I asked as I noticed myself becoming a little irritated by the silliness of it all.

The only answer I got was a big smile, a bow and, "I must leave you here for a guide, six inches taller than myself, who will guide you a further sixty paces towards the His Excellency's chapel. You are expected." With that he walked swiftly away so my question was not really answered.

"Not claustrophobic, are you young lady?" asked a voice close to me. Turning I saw a man, also dressed in a black cloak covering him from head to feet, smiling at me.

"Er, no, I don't think so." Before I could think what else to ask, I was following the person as I had the others. Are you six inches taller than?" but I did not finish.

"Six inches taller, I am and proud of the fact I be," he answered, not bothering to look back at me.

"Down we go," he said as he led me to a small door in the stone wall. "Lower you head that you may pass through this door. We now journey downwards."

"But I don't want to go down," I called out, but the man had already disappeared through the door. "Come, come," he called back at me, "down the steps and soon we will be there."

Concerned I was being asked to walk down a number of stone steps with very little light, I called out, "where are we going?"

"Fifty- eight, fifty-nine, sixty," he called out as if talking to himself. "Here we are, now we must we wait for his Excellency's guide."

"Will he be six inches taller,?" I asked.

"Of course. Of course, tradition is important. One should always follow the rules."

Not understanding anything being said, I was about to turn and make my way back when another person nudged my elbow. "This way Miss Jemima," Turning, I saw another similarly dressed very old man holding a candlestick. Containing a long candle, he turned away from me and walked on, holding the candlestick in front of him, lighting up the way ahead. Walking on, all I could do was to follow him and hope someone would offer some explanation where I was being taken.

A short while later, he announced, "a few steps here." He then proceeded to make his way carefully up each one as I noticed a few were missing, so had to carefully climb over the gaps. Following him, the way was easier as there appeared to be more light coming from somewhere, but still wondering how my name was known to these people.

"In here Miss, you should bow your head upon entering." He paused, then added, "It is only polite and you only need to do it once."

Completely mystified, I followed him as he stopped at a door. Waiting then listening to what might be happening behind the door, he waited a further short while, then knocking, slowly opened the door and made his way through the open doorway.

"Pray enter and welcome my child," called out a voice from the far side of the room. Peering inside and slightly nervous, I slowly walked a few paces into the darkened room. Stopping behind the guide who had also stopped, I waited wondering where I could be.

Bowing low, the guide peered towards me. Remembering what had been said, I also bowed my head still not understanding why.

"Your excellency, may I present."

"Yes, yes, I am aware of the young lady's name." Looking at me, he announced, "Miss Jemima Jones. Please come forward that I might see you. There are only candles in this chapel so you must come closer my dear that I may see and talk to you."

"I am not sure why I am here or how you know my name," I said, "but I am on a visit and thought I should," but I did not finish.

"Usher, stand aside that I might see more clearly with the aid of these few candles, this young lady's face."

As the person moved to one side, I walked a few paces forward. In front of me, I saw a tall elderly man dressed in a long purple cloak with a purple cap upon his head. Smiling at me, he said, "I have arranged for you to meet me to thank you for your valuable assistance in securing that most important relic, the sacred cup."

"The sacred cup," I repeated, wondering what was meant, then added, "oh, the relic."

"The relic indeed, young lady. Abbott Joshua is elderly as we all have become over the years. The terrible journey through that night of storms did little to help his condition, but it did not harm his mission. The Abbott has explained perhaps the history of the relic?"

"Yes," I replied. "I believe it was originally from an ancient temple and saved from those attacking the temple. I believe it has since been hidden throughout the centuries."

"And will be hidden again. The time is coming when an important religious festival will be upon us. Perhaps the most important festival at which time the sacred object will be passed to one who will again hide it that it may be protected as the Abbott and his ancestors have protected it. You will, I trust, understand the importance of what I am saying."

"Yes, sir, I mean, your excellency," wondering if I should mention about the item was now in the grain basket.

"I am also aware of your problems and have faith in your efforts."

There was a silence as I wondered if I should say anything.

"Now, we come to why you are here."

"Yes, sir?"

"When you have secured the relic and are assured of your safety, I refer to those who would rob you of the item. You shall take it in secret and with regard to your own safety, to where last you met the Abbott."

"In a room, I thought to be a crypt in Christchurch Priory was where I last met him," I said.

"Precisely, there you will be reunited with the Abbott. It is my wish and the wish of all of us here that you then arrange passage to the village of Sopley. There to the watermill where members of my sect will make themselves known to you. You will, of course, make this journey in the greatest secrecy."

"Arrange passage, sir?"

"Arrange passage. The last important task asked of you. Then will you be free to decide to return to the circus for the remainder of your holiday or leave and continue your holiday elsewhere."

Unable to think what I should say, I was silent for a moment then as I was about to say something, the person smiled at me and indicated to the usher, still holding out his candlestick, that the meeting was over. Walking towards me, the man indicated I was to follow him, which is what I did. As I reached the door, I turned to see the person again, but he had disappeared. Looking around the smallish chapel, there appeared to be no other doors or windows. Confused, I heard the usher say gently, "this way Miss, the meeting is over. I will lead you to a nearby door and the outside world."

Turning and following him, I was led to through a narrow passage towards what I thought must be the church wall. As we became closer, I could make out in the gloom, a small door in the stone wall. As I became closer, the door opened, letting in the light which flooded the passageway.

"Thank you for coming, Miss," said a voice behind me.

Crouching down and walking through the open doorway, I could see I was now outside the surrounding wall of the church. The door slammed itself shut and I was now alone. Waiting a short while as I tried to work out where I must now be, I walked on following the wall until I came very close to the entrance gate. Looking again up at the impressive cathedral as it towered high over the neighbouring houses, I made my way back to the market square where I was pleased to see my friends and Carrie-Ann sitting on benches, chattering and I suppose, waiting for me to return.

During the return journey, my thoughts were occupied with getting back to the tents containing the grain baskets as quickly as possible and hopefully without attracting any undue attention, to search and find the relic.

Leaving the transport outside the circus area, I again waited behind, in case Carrie-Ann needed any help with her wheelchair, but she was obviously used to being in similar situations, so we were soon both on our way to our caravan.

Having neared the caravan, she suddenly remembered she had promised to see someone concerning a decision that had to be made, immediately on returning. Seeing her go, I realised this left me free to continue my task without having to make any excuses.

The tent containing the feed baskets was deserted as I would have expected as the ponies were feed only at certain times of the day. Drawing the tent door flap from the entrance, I began my search. Shifting each basket to a new position so I would know which ones I had already searched, gave me the excuse to say I was in the tent for a reason should anyone appear. The first searches were uneventful and I looked desperately at the remaining baskets, there seemed so many.

It was when I was about to search the tenth basket that I thought I heard the sound of someone near the tent. Rearranging the grain in the basket and standing back, I heard the tent flap open as a person came a little way into the tent.

"Oh, do excuse me please. I am a little lost. This is not the tent where I will find the owner of the circus?" a voice called out.

Looking to the entrance, I was appalled to see the same person I had first seen on the marsh, while excising the pony a few days ago." Thinking quickly what to say and to hide my nervousness, I said, "oh no, you will have to see Mrs Hibbard. She will know where that person is, but her caravan is far from here."

Coming in a few steps, he continued, "why I do believe you are the same young lady I met that early morning on the marshes. You perhaps do not remember me although it was not very long ago. I was enquiring as to the whereabouts of a former associate. I was concerned and I am still concerned as to his welfare. I have asked around the area and several people have been quite helpful, but none have been able to assist my enquiries. However, someone did think they had seen you walking across the recreation ground about that time. I do so hope you might be able to assist me, even in the smallest possible way. As I believe I mentioned previously when I met you, my only concern is as to the welfare of the person I am seeking, bearing in mind his age and condition."

"With so many people gathering to see the circus preparations," I quickly replied, "I am not sure which person you could be referring to but, if I," the man quickly interrupted me.

"I will remain in the area and I am sure our paths will cross again. Perhaps, if that happens, you will be able to assist me on that occasion."

"Perhaps so," I replied.

Looking down at the basket nearest me, he said, "I assume you are quite busy, arranging the feed for the animals. Perhaps, while I am here, I might help you in some way."

"Thank you for your offer," I quickly replied. "I have nearly finished and as you see, there is nothing here except the animal feed and other items needed for their bedding."

"Of course, of course," he replied. "Remember, I won't be far away should you suddenly remember anything, anything at all." And with that he left the tent, leaving the door flap wide open.

Waiting awhile, but then swiftly making my way to the entrance to the tent, I closed the flap and secured it from the inside so no-one could enter.

Now I was not sure what to do. I had to find the relic, but then I would have to hide it quickly in a more secure place and without being seen. Turning my attention to the next basket, then the next, I finally dug my hand into the grain of a basket and felt something very hard and very warm. Withdrawing my hand, I concentrated on what I had to do and most important where I could hide the relic. Plunging my hand again into the soft grain, I pulled out the object and immediately wrapped it in a nearby towel, used to rub down the ponies. Then picking up a small blanket used under saddles, I wrapped it around the towel. Then unfastening the flap fixings, I opened it just slightly to see outside the tent.

Not far away, another tent used for storing props but not yet full, was close by. Making my way quickly there, I determined I would stay out of the open as much as possible. Finally, after going from tent to tent I was very near to my caravan. Almost running the short distance, I was relieved to see Carrie-Ann had not yet returned and so had ample time to chose a sufficient place to hide the relic. The only place I could think of was under my own pillow. Then I decided to remove the pillow cover and place the relic within the pillow, with a few small cushions over it to hide the bulge as much as possible.

In a short time, Carrie-Ann appeared and I was able to relax a little, knowing I was now more secure and safe.

A little while later as we both were thinking about leaving the caravan for high tea, I realised the relic was not as safe as I would like it to be, so looked around the caravan for a better hiding place. As Carrie-Ann left the caravan, I suggested I would join her in a few minutes. During that time, I looked and looked and finally settled on a small place behind a number of heavy books I had never seen used. When I was satisfied with that arrangement, I left the caravan and joined the others, looking forward to high tea.

Chapter Ten

A river trip to a water mill and
another meeting with a 'King'.

I determined the next morning to seek Carrie-Ann's help. Without telling her of all the details, I did just mention I was looking after something very special for someone and was concerned the item might be stolen should someone enter the caravan in our absence.

"That is easily achieved, I lock the caravan door when I am not here and there are always circus people around who will know when strangers are in this area."

Relieved again, I joined her for breakfast and discussed taking the pony to the marsh for the usual morning exercise.

"All settled," she said, "and we can talk about anything else you want to talk about concerning this mysterious thing you are guarding for this mysterious person you mentioned."

Satisfied, I walked towards the animal shelter and made ready to take the Shetland pony across the marshes. Once there and while I was very close to the far end of the marsh, that I noticed a small craft being guided by a man and coming across the river from the direction of Christchurch Quay and will, very likely, pass close to me.

"Hello there young lady," he called out as the boat drew closer. "Saw you walking across the marsh as I was docking at Christchurch quay earlier," he shouted as his small craft glided silently across the surface of the river. Guiding it slowly towards a narrow sandbank, he stopped the craft to stop very close to the edge of the marsh. "Bill Forster again," he called out, "and how are you today?"

Pleased to see him, I replied, "as you can see, I am exercising the pony which I do most early mornings." Leaving the pony munching on a small area of grass, I crossed over a small stream to be nearer to the boat. "This is the river Avon, isn't it?" I asked.

"About this point," he replied, "there are two rivers and they both join a short way back there before flowing into the harbour."

"Someone told me the river that is the Avon goes towards Ringwood town, but on the way, also flows past the watermill in Sopley village and it is possible to use the river to go between the two places."

"That is correct, rowed it myself a few times," he replied

"You have rowed from here to the watermill?" I asked, a little excitedly. "Is it fairly easy?"

"Yes and even further upstream to Ringwood, but it is not that easy or straightforward. You first need to be aware of a few things."

"Oh," was all I said. Then, thinking about it asked, "is it difficult?"

"That depends, why do you ask, thinking of having a go yourself?" he joked.

"No, I did think as the river travels from here and past the mill on it's journey to that town you mentioned, it might be a way for me to think about," then I paused. "What are the things a person needs to know?" "The first thing to think about is the type of boat used, that is important.

The water depth and bridge clearance are also things to consider. You need to make sure the boat can pass under any bridges without hitting them and hopefully when the tide is in, so there is more water below the boat and less chance of hitting anything in the water. The Avon is a public navigable waterway and in some parts, it is also a private fishery. Some people do not want you to sail on what they regard as their river, even though it is your right. And then a favourable wind is a bonus. If it is against you, the journey can be very tiring."

Thinking about all this, I said, "it all seems very complicated. I was hoping there might be a way to reach the watermill at Sopley village by the river Avon, but I suppose not."

"Don't be too disappointed. Rowing upstream can be done with patience. I can do it any day of the week, but as I have said, it is easier when conditions are right. If I might enquire, is there an important reason why you are asking?"

"Can I take you into my confidence?" I asked, lowering my voice slightly, even though I knew the marsh was almost deserted.

"The aforesaid Mr William Foster can be relied on to respect a confidence especially if it is important. Is it important?"

"Yes," I quickly replied.

"Is it very important?"

"Yes," I again answered.

"But is it very, very important, so important that something special can only be achieved by doing whatever it is you want to do?" he asked.

"Yes, I believe so."

"Then Mr William Foster, also known as 'Bill' is your man. What exactly is it you want to do?"

Hesitating at first, then slowly I said, "an elderly man has an important item he needs to pass onto someone near the watermill in Sopley village, although I am not sure where that might be. I do know he must be taken to that mill."

"And is there a problem, apart from the problems of using a boat to get to the watermill near Sopley village?"

"No, no problem. Well, actually, there is another person who wants to take this item away and have it for himself, but I have been very careful to see he does not know where I am."

"I see, so it is not, you will excuse the expression, plain sailing."

"No," I answered, feeling a little guilty.

"And when is this event to take place?" he asked.

"I was told when I enter the town priory, the elderly man will be available, so as soon as possible. I have already lost the relic when I had it in my care once and I nearly lost it a second time. I must get the elderly man to the watermill as quickly as possible so he will be in no danger."

"And if this all took place and nothing happened to stop us making our way and we all arrived at the watermill, what then?"

"Then the elderly man will be taken care of by friends and we will return, hopefully by the river."

"I see. I am intrigued and you are in luck because I have finished my work for today. As I would not want to see this old man, you speak of, come to any harm, I will help you. It should not be too difficult and will be an interesting adventure. However, as to time, soon might be sensible as there is a fog coming in from the sea, which is why I finished my work early. It will probably cover the harbour and the marshes late this afternoon, but could be here before then." Then thinking, he added, "you said there was a person who also wanted this thing you mentioned?"

"Yes," I answered.

"In that case, the fog will very usefully hide us in this area and once we had gone a certain distance along the river, that person will no longer be a threat to anyone. There will be no way of him following us, you can be sure of that."

Pausing, he made ready to drag his boat off the sandbank. "That's it then, today or never. You said the elderly man is presently in the priory. I have a shallow boat that will be ideal for the journey and can take three people. I will be ready for you as soon as I have gone home and let my people know when I shall be returning."

"Thank you so much," I said, nervous at my new responsibility. "I feel so relieved. I looked forward to meeting you again very soon."

"You know the old building known as the 'Norman House' by the old bridge?" he asked.

"Oh yes," I replied, "I have walked past it many times."

"I will be hidden and moored under the first arch of the old bridge. Make your way there along the stream, where the trees will hide you, then towards the bridge. You will see me waiting under the first arch." With that he used one oar to finally push his boat further away from the narrow sandbank and waving goodbye, continued rowing towards

Mudeford Quay.

Holding the reins of the pony, I made my way back across the marsh and back to the circus relieved that at last, I could see an end to my task, although I thought, I hoped to continue being with the circus for the remainder of the summer holidays.

Taking Carrie-Ann into my confidence, I was pleased to see her reaction, as the first thing she said was, "if you are going to make that journey, I was arrange for our cook to make a selection of sandwiches for the three of you."

Thanking her, I then revealed where I had hidden the relic.

Offering me a bag and saying, "it is a very strange looking thing."

Wrapping the relic in an old newspaper and placing it at the bottom of the bag, I then rolled up a few towels, placing them over the item, seeking to further hide it.

"Good luck," called out Carrie-Ann. "Try not to be too late back, but I will wait up for you in case you are delayed."

Thanking her and with the long strap of the bag wrapped tightly around my shoulder, I made my way with a note for the cook about the sandwiches to take with me.

A short while later I was on my way towards the priory church with the relic and sandwiches. Looking around me, in case I was being watched or followed, I quickly walked along Bridge street, past the Norman House and along the narrow walkway following the stream. Walking towards the priory church, I turned and quickly skipped through the graveyard and quickly into the priory, conscious of how nervous I was feeling. Walking quickly towards the place where I had last seen the elderly Abbott, I began to wonder what I would do if he was not there or could not hear me. I tried to banish all negative thoughts from my head and concentrate on what I was supposed to be doing.

Stopping at the part of the side aisle by the small door under the main altar, I knocked on the door, at the same time looking around and wishing my knock was not so loud. Fortunately there appeared to be no visitors in this part of the aisle. Waiting, there was no response. Knocking again, I waited for the door to be swung open and the figure of the Abbott greeting me. Instead, there was again no response from behind the door. Standing back as I felt I might be too conspicuous crouching close to the door, I walked to the other side of the aisles and again waited, my thoughts racing as I became more concerned.

Wondering what I should do, I thought only to quickly walk to the far end of the church and then, passing under the 'Miraculous Beam,' make my way along the other aisles in case the Abbott should be waiting for me there. Then I tried to remember all that the person in Salisbury Cathedral had told me. Perhaps I had the wrong date, but then, I could not remember any date being mentioned. As I walked past the first of the small chapels built into the side of the altar, a voice whispered my name. Looking around and feeling my heart beating, I could see no-one. Hearing my name called out a second time, I peered into the nearest small chapel. On the lower part I could see an arm reaching out to me.

"My dear, in here. Stay where you are. I shall join you." Standing back, I waited as to my immense relief, the Abbott struggled to climb out of the small opening. "My dear, you have the sacred relic?" he asked, seeming as concerned as I was feeling.

"Yes sir, I mean Abbott Joshua. It is in my bag and I have a tight grip on the strap."
"I awaited you my dear, but danger came first. I could feel it. I knew to not open the door where I was to meet you. I could feel the presence of

one who had somehow discovered my retreat. Come now we must depart. To where I know not, but to safety, surely."

A
s

"I followed the path alongside the priory."

Taking the Abbott's arm, I led him quickly to the main entrance, being concerned as to his ability to walk more quickly than he could safely walk. Once almost outside the priory church, I waited as I searched around the graveyard for any sign of the younger abbot. Seeing only a few visitors, with a few sitting on the benches eating their sandwiches, I pulled the Abbott gently to the right, following the path alongside the priory north side. Quickly, we made our way along to the path and towards the narrow stream.

Following the stream and passing the cover offered by the trees, I paused as we were now exposed in the open. Gently pulling the Abbott's arm, we walked on and were soon past the Norman House. Looking across to the old bridge, I could see no sign of Bill Foster and his boat, which caused me to feel more nervous than I already was.

Walking quickly towards the first arch and leaving the Abbott a few steps behind me, I crouched down and peered into the gloom. With the greatest relief, I could see Bill Foster waiting for us in a small boat nearer the rear of the arch.

The old Norman bridge where a boat awaited us.
Seeing me, he called out and using his hands to push against the arch wall, guided the boat towards me, holding it steady. Seeing the Abbott, for the first time, he held out his hand to guide the old man into the middle of the boat. Then I made my way in as he first steadied the boat, then picking up an oar, used it to push us all further away from the wall. Rowing, he guided the boat into the wider part of the river where he was able to use both oars to row the boat quickly along the river.

"The tide is with us and the water deep," he called out, "shouldn't be too difficult, although there is as yet, no sign of the fog."

While the Abbott settled himself down, I clutched the bag still strapped to me and looked out at the passing scenery as we made out way along the river.

After awhile and feeling myself and the Abbott no longer in any danger, I relaxed, turned and looked back at the bridge. There on the bridge, I thought I saw the younger Abbott standing and shouting at us. Thinking it best not to alert the elderly man sitting just in front of me, I resumed looking at and admiring the changing river scenery with the swans and herons swimming and flying past us.

My admiration of the passing scenery was sometimes interrupted by my head falling forwards as I momentary fell sleep only to be awakened by the sound of something. On one occasion, I noticed the river divided into two streams. Fortunately, Bill knew the correct stream to take. "The other one leads to a weir for the waterworks company," he called back to me. What I did notice was how often the river seemed to just meander along the flat open grounds. There seemed to be twists and turns everywhere as if a long straight river had been twisted so that anyone travelling along it would take twice as long as the journey should. Gazing to my left I could look up to the top of St Catherine's Hill. I remember that many years ago, the original builders of the priory church had wanted to build it on the top of that hill and the decision to build it close to the marshes, was the origin of the 'miraculous beam' story and legend.

"Passing the village of Winkton, soon," called out Bill, "this whole valley is a flood plane when the river floods," he explained. Then added, "Sopley Mill will be next when we leave the main river and take the narrow stream, built to service the mill."

I had forgotten about the Abbott, but he just sat very still and said little, so I just hoped his ordeal would soon be over.

In no time at all, we approached the mill building, when Bill called out, "we can stop anywhere along this bank and leave the boat here for our return."

Sorry to leave the boat, I stepped off onto the grassy bank, then turned to help the Abbott as he struggled to stand up. "Thank you my dear," he said and holding my arm. "I survived that night of storms so can survive this journey," Then he was soon out and gingerly walking a few steps.

"What now?" called out Bill, looking back at the two of us as he pulled the boat higher onto the riverbank.

"I believe someone in the mill is expecting us," I replied, trying to remember exactly what I had been told in the cathedral in Salisbury town. As we approached the mill, suddenly the door was flung open and two men, each dressed in a long black clock, buttoned up at the front, walked the short distance towards us, bowed, then smiling, one said, "Your excellency, we wish you welcome, senior members of our order await you in the nearby chapel of 'St Michael and All Angels'. It is just a short distance yonder."

As the Abbott stepped forward, the other person said, "today is an important day for all of us." Then walking away, one said, "please follow us to the parish church." As we all walked up the slight hill and turned into the main path of the church, one of the two men turned and said, "your excellency, our dignitaries await you within this chapel with great joy in their hearts. May we thank your two companions for assisting you here. They may now be released from the task which has resulted in your presence here today."

With that the Abbott, letting go of my arm turned to me saying, "my dear, you have helped my immensely. The very reason I first came to the priory church in Christchurch village on that dreadful night was to transfer to others, now inside this small parish church, the sacred relic you now carry. It could not take place in that priory church as the purpose of my visit was later discovered by those who would take this sacred relic for their own purpose. I am now here in this almost hidden church to continue that task, as are all of us and away from prying eyes."

At that moment, thinking about the strange encounter with two men and the approach to the church, I had almost forgotten about the relic. Taking the strap of the bag from my arm, I carefully removed the towels hiding the object, then carefully removed the relic from the bag, feeling a little embarrassed about the newspaper covering it, as all eyes seemed to be on what I was doing.

At that moment a third man, dressed as were the other two, emerged from the door of the small chapel and carrying a purple cushion, stood before me, holding it up. As I carefully placed the relic on the cushion, the man then held the cushion with one hand and covered the relic with a purple cloth. Looking at the group, he turned and slowly made his way back through the main door of the church.

Sopley parish church.

"His Excellency awaits you inside," said one of the men, almost in a whisper.

"Of course, of course," repeated the Abbot. Turning to me, he said, "I must now join the others, my dear. He who has been stalking me will no longer trouble you, as it will be made known there is now no further chance of him gaining for himself, or for others, that which he has for so long tried to steal. Again, thank you for all the help you have given me." Turning he walked into the church with the others, leaving Bill and myself outside and alone.

Waiting a few minutes, Bill, looking at me then asked, "well, what now? Journey back home, I suppose."

"Yes," I replied, then putting my hand in my bag, exclaimed, "I forgot the sandwiches, my friend in the circus arranged for us to have sandwiches for our journey."

"That's alright then," said Bill, "we can return to where we left the boat, sit on the riverbank and eat the sandwiches. It will be a picnic on a lovely summers day to crown a job well done."

Happy to agree with him, we both left the church, set off down the slight slope towards to where we had left the boat, made ourselves comfortable and enjoyed both the sight of herons diving into the river and the views of the countryside. Even the watermill made little noise to disturb the peaceful setting.

Regretfully, the time to make the return journey came all too soon. Pulling the boat back into the river, Bill held it steady as I carefully stepped inside and made myself as comfortable as I was able and even though he had said very little, I began to miss the presence of the Abbott.

The return journey was as uneventful as it was relaxing. Even the continual twisting and turning of the river as the boat made it's way slowly onward, often passing a stretch of the river we had just left, so close where the meandering curves of the river. Finally we returned to the attractive pool before the old bridge from where we had parted. "Leave you here?" asked Bill, "it's about as close as I can get to he recreation ground, I can even hear the music coming from the circus, or it might be the funfair."

Making my way out of the boat with Bill helping me onto the shore, I looked around at the attractive scene before me. The Old Norman House and the Norman priory church rising up behind it and the tranquility of the silently flowing river. Even the two fishermen sitting idly in a shallow boat, anchored to the river bed, were as silent as they could be, not wanting to disturb the fish.

"Get any more tasks like that," called out Bill, I think joking, "you will know where I live on Mudeford Quay."

"Thank you again," I called out. "Assisting the old man would not have been possible without your help."

"Bye," he called out as he set off past the priory church and the many yachts sitting along side the river's edge and onto the Quay.

Watching him go and relieved the fog did not appear, I turned and was about to make my way back to the circus, when I heard my name being called out. "Jemima." The sound came from the far end off the bridge, so I could not yet see who was calling me. Making my way up the bank and onto the road, I was immediately relieved to see the familiar figure of Carrie-Ann in her wheelchair.

"Glad to see you have returned safe and sound," she called out. "I trust everything worked out as you hoped it would."

"Yes," I replied. "I am so glad the whole business is finished and I can now relax and just concentrate of enjoying my time whilst with the circus during the remaining part of the holiday."

"And we will be very happy to have you stay with us," she replied, which made me even more relaxed, knowing I could continue working with the animals and seeing all my new friends.

"I am on my way to Priory House to see about the funfair arrangements," she added. "I will be there for some time. If, once you have rested, you might like to join me, but if you are feeling tired after your adventure, we can meet again later."

"Thank you," I replied, a little unsure of what to do as seeing the clock on the priory tower, I noted it was still only the middle of the afternoon. "As it is only a short distance away," I called after her. "I am not too tired, the river journey was relaxing, so I could join you now. I only have this bag to carry."

"Excellent," she said, "put the bag in the back of the wheelchair and you won't need to carry it."
The short journey back to the lawn of Priory House took us both past

the entrance to the priory church and I thought of how, only a few hours previously, I was nervously guiding an elderly man along the same path to the old Norman bridge. How everything now seemed so peaceful and relaxed.

Carries-Ann announced she would first like to talk to a person about progress on the funfair about whatever else might be needed. I decided to make my way to the far part of the lawn and past Priory House.

Walking past the house, I noticed by the front door a rather portly gentleman dressed in clothes I don't believe I had ever seen before. Upon his head, he wore a large hat with a wide brim and two feathers hanging from the top, Looking down, a large sword was strapped to his side and his knee length boots shone in the sun. He had a large smile on his face as he beamed at me.

"My dear," he called out, "you have returned to congratulate me on the good news I have received just this very morning."

"Sir?" I asked.

"My return, you have heard the news. My throne is vacant, the usurper has been banished and my good people desire earnestly my immediate return. My people love me, in towns and countryside, they are ready to flock to me. I, Louis the eighteenth am about to fulfill my destiny. Today, France will again have a monarch. This very day I sail back to my country to be once again united with my countrymen. You are obviously pleased for me as I see you have hurried to congratulate me."

"Sir, of course I do," I quickly replied, not understanding anything the gentleman was saying. Then I paused wondering what I should say. Thinking back to when I had first visited this house, I was sure the gentlemen to be coming out of the large mirror. Perhaps I had imagined it. Continuing, I added, "Sir, I thought you to be, I mean when I saw you coming from that mirror."

"An illusion, my dear young lady, an illusion. Go now, my staff even now await me as I travel to the harbour to board ship to my country. From there, I shall board a larger ship that will take me to a French harbour" With that, he waved his hand and as two similarly dressed men appeared behind him, rushing to his side, the three walked off very quickly, I suppose to Christchurch Quay, a short distance away.

Again confused, as I seemed so often to be, I walked across the far part of the lawn admiring the funfair attractions already set up and awaiting the opening date when all attractions will be ready for the town's children to enjoy for the remainder of the holidays.

When Carrie-Ann had finished inspecting the work already carried out and the few items remaining, we both set out for the pleasant journey back to the circus.

"We will both be in time for high tea," she reminded me, "I trust you did enjoy the sandwiches cook made for your adventure."

"Yes, they were very welcome" I said and looked forward to being once more enjoying the remainder of my holidays with the circus. Will I have anything to tell my friends when I return to St Peter's school? I asked myself. I don't suppose any of my friends would really believe me.

THE END

Printed in Great Britain
by Amazon